BOOKS BY SUZA KATES

The Savannah Coven Series
Whisper of a Witch
Conviction of a Witch
Binding of a Witch
Haunting of a Witch
Possession of a Witch
Deception of a Witch
Suffering of a Witch
Boys' Night Out (E-novella)
Vengeance of a Witch
Sacrifice of a Witch

The Sisters' Grimoire Series
The Sisters' Grimoire (Novella)

Single Titles
Hallowed Eve
The Penance Stone
She Who is Hidden

Coming 2015
Watchtower Maidens Series
Call to the East
(Turn the page for a preview!)

The SISTERS' GRIMOIRE

SUZA KATES

ICASM PRESS
SAVANNAH

Published by Icasm Publishing LLC
5710 Ogeechee Rd. Suite 200 #278, Savannah, GA 31405
www.icasmpress.com

Library of Congress Cataloging-in-Publication Data

Kates, Suza
The Sisters' Grimoire / Suza Kates
     p. cm.

ISBN-13:978-1-9423180-6-4 (ebook)
ISBN-13:978-1-9423180-6-4 (ebook)
I. Title

Printed and bound in the United States of America

10 9 8 7 6 5 4 3 2 1

A huge thanks to David, Mandi, and Donna for all of their hard work!

1

Flames danced in the kitchen fireplace, framed by an arch of ivory-painted bricks. Holding her hands to the heat, Tate Whiteburn sat on the hearth and listened to the patter of soft yet insistent rain.

She'd returned to her hometown of Bar Harbor, Maine this morning, only to be met by an autumn storm and its iron-sky welcome. With the cold outside, she should have been soothed by the glow of orange and yellow embers.

But she was too distracted, glancing every few minutes to the door, expecting it to open.

She spread her fingers to gather warmth. Curled them again to hold it.

Where is she?

The wind moaned as it rolled around the corner of the white house, rattling the shutters as it passed. The gale was little more than a bully issuing a parting threat, as the four-story Victorian had stood firm near the cliffs since 1905.

Tate wrinkled her brow, but not because of the howling gusts and splattering rain. Her only concern was for Fiona's tender feelings. The possibility they'd be crushed grew with every tick of the clock.

Tate had flown in and still made it in plenty of time. So where was Sami?

"Did you hear that wind?" Fiona strolled into the kitchen and veered her course to the bay window with a view of the front yard. A swift gust kicked up to slap droplets against the glass just as lightning branched a pure-white vein across the black.

Fiona jumped when thunder crashed.

Laughing at herself, she ran a hand over her sleek cap of raven hair and turned to Tate. "It's getting worse out there. I hope Sami's all right."

"I'm sure she's fine. Just running late." Tate reassured her youngest sister. She twisted her mouth, tried to bite down, but couldn't stop herself from adding, "You know Sami."

"Tate . . ." Fiona said, filling her voice with a plea for peace.

Drawing a deep breath, Tate searched for a way to change the topic. She walked over to study the lop-sided birthday cake she'd made. Two tiers of chocolate cake with vanilla frosting—tinted purple, Fiona's favorite color—and topped with barely-legible writing.

The white gobs ringing the edges were supposed to be roses. "I know you're the chef around here," she said, "but I wanted to do something special."

Fiona beamed at the off-kilter layers. "I'm sure it will taste wonderful." She crossed to Tate, took her hand. "But you're home, so my day's already special."

Tate reached to tug on Fiona's hair, an old habit, but the raven braids were long-gone. "You're supposed to be the spoiled brat, Fee. The baby. How is it you're always the peacemaker?"

Fiona's head kicked back as she laughed. "Because you and Sami give me plenty of practice."

Again Tate pressed her lips together, wishing she'd held her tongue before. She swore to do so for the rest of the night and avoid any confrontation with Sami. She would gift Fiona some sibling harmony on her birthday.

They both turned when the door burst open. The storm's furious clamor breached their cozy nest for a moment before the rain-drenched figure slammed the door shut.

Sami had arrived, and just in time.

Though she sported a yellow slicker over the haggard cords and flannel she wore for work, wetness darkened the long curls that had escaped the hood, turning the tips of her auburn hair to mahogany. Her deep brown eyes were the exact shade of Tate's, a trait passed to them by their Romanian grandmother.

Those gypsy eyes smoothly tracked the room to assess the situation, then Sami flipped back the hood and winked at Fiona. "Hey, kid."

Fiona's smile was radiant, as if Sami had brought her a basket of sunshine instead of a wet mess on the floor. "You made it!"

Sami performed her one-shoulder shrug, her favorite response to . . . almost everything. "Did you ever doubt?"

"Actually . . ." Tate split the low ponytail of her own black hair into two pieces and tightened with a quick yank. "It's ten 'til midnight, Sami. I'm glad you decided to squeeze us into your schedule."

Sami's bright grin remained but hardened around the edges. "I don't keep schedules, Tate. That's your thing, remember?"

Frustration stirred beneath Tate's outward calm, a familiar annoyance bearing Sami's unique watermark. "What were you doing so late at night?"

"Working."

"Working. And this project couldn't wait?"

"No. It couldn't." Sami slid out of her raincoat and let it plop to the floor in a sodden heap. Eyes sparking, she pointed her finger at Tate.

Then the fire in her gaze dimmed. The hand fell. "I don't want to argue. We hardly see you enough as it is to waste the time."

Tate doubted the comment was meant as a barb, but the reminder of her absence still pricked her conscience. "You're right." She swallowed against a constricting throat. "I'm sorry for jumping on you."

Fiona walked between them and bent to pick up the raincoat.

Sami grimaced as she kneeled to scoop it up. "Sorry, Fee. You don't have to pick up after me."

Fiona tilted her head and feigned surprise. "Really? Since when?"

"Since," Sami had the good sense to look chagrined, "it's your birthday." She stepped into the mudroom to hang up her coat. When she came back out, she was all smiles again. "Speaking of which." She pulled her phone from a pocket and held it out to Fiona. "Happy birthday."

Fiona studied the image on the screen. "Oh, your piece. Is this what you've been making? It's so fluid. Solid but soft. It's . . . it's . . ." Fiona stalled, scrunching her nose. "What is it?"

"The picture's small, so it's hard to tell, but all total, it measures about two-by-five and is meant to hang on a wall. I made it for your shop."

Tate moved in and examined the photo alongside her sisters. "What shop?"

"Yes," Fiona's head popped up, "what shop?"

Sami lifted a shoulder. "The one you're always talking about opening. You've shown me the color scheme a hundred times, so I knew the pastels would work."

This was why Sami had been late. She'd been finishing Fiona's birthday present.

Shame pricked at the base of Tate's skull and heated her face. "It's perfect," she said, sending Sami an apology with her eyes.

The collage featured a pink cupcake with sprinkles, a slice of cheesecake, and other colorful confections all melded into a piece of art. The visual was cheery, whimsical, and brought lazy Sunday afternoons to mind.

It also shifted Tate's sweet-loving taste buds into overdrive.

Sami was good at what she did, and her mind worked in brilliant ways, turning misshapen hunks of iron and other metals into sheer beauty. She possessed an aptitude for metallurgy and a flair for design.

Just as their mother had.

"It's beautiful, Sami." Fiona put a palm to her chest. "But I'm still only dreaming. I don't have a place to hang this yet."

"Part two of your birthday present." Now Sami looked smug. "I happen to know there's a property on High Street coming up for rental soon. I called Joan Wilson and made an appointment for you to have a look."

"And you call *me* pushy. However," Tate added when Sami scowled, "I happen to agree. You've been saving and planning for so long, Fee. Maybe the timing is finally right."

Fiona swiveled her head back and forth between her sisters, pausing occasionally to stare at the photo.

Tate knew the moment she made up her mind, because she sighed, her expression turning all soft and dreamy. "Well, I guess it couldn't hurt to look."

"Yes!" Sami pumped a fist.

"Just look," Fiona said. But she jumped up and down a few times before handing over the phone. "Now I'm really ready for some cake."

"Me too." Sami angled around them and headed for the long rectangle of the antique table. She stopped short when she saw the cake. "Who made that?"

As they watched, a gobby white rose slid down one side.

"Who do you think?" Tate's sharp gaze dared her to criticize further.

"It looks . . . purple." Sami gave her a half-smile. "It's good to see you, Tate. Been a long time."

Tate relayed a new version of her usual excuse. "I've had a busy year. I'm editing a textbook meant for post-graduate classes. The Medieval Society."

Fiona hummed acceptance. "Sounds interesting."

Sami said nothing.

Suddenly uncomfortable, Tate nodded and glanced back to the cake. Her sisters knew the real reason she stayed away, and the pretext rang false, even to her.

Turning back to the fire, Tate pretended to warm her hands.

But it was her heart that felt the bitter chill.

Being in this sad, haunted house was simply too painful. Every room, every smell, reminded her of their mother. After twenty years, the wound should have healed. The ache should have faded.

But the family home and quaint city of Bar Harbor somehow fed her mother's spirit. The nostalgia kept her alive, though always out of reach.

This was why Tate had left. Not to hurt her sisters.

But to save herself.

A photo sat on the mantel above, the last picture taken of their mother. She was smiling at the camera, holding a two-year-old Fiona on her hip. Both of them shone with the happiness of a secure and promising life.

Two weeks later, their mother was dead.

Grief was a jagged shard of glass in Tate's chest, cutting and slicing as it always did when she came home. *I only have to make it through the night.*

First thing in the morning, she'd be on a plane, leaving behind the sorrow—and her family—once again.

Fiona's easy laughter drifted across the kitchen, drawing Tate's attention to where she stood with Sami. The three of them all came from the same stock, but their shared loss had contributed so much to their personalities, to their unique natures.

Three broken little branches, now grown in different directions.

Sami noticed Tate watching them and paused. She gave her the smile she always did when she knew Tate's thoughts wandered a somber path.

Then she brightened, snapping her fingers and pointing finger-guns at Fee. "It's 11:54." She whipped out a lighter from her pocket. "Almost time."

Tate steeled her face into a happy expression, camouflage for her wounded heart. "I'll call Granddad and Brit."

"We're already here," her grandfather said as he and Uncle Brit strolled in from the front parlor. At sixty-five, Granddad had the silver hair of an older man, but the spry, athletic body of one half his age. The ornate cane of silver and wood in his hand was always with him, but never used.

"All three of you together." He beamed, taking in the sight of the girls he'd raised after his daughter's passing. "Birthdays and holidays don't come often enough."

Brit walked over to chuck Fiona's chin. "Happy birthday, little Fee." The two of them could have been male and female bookends with their black-as-midnight hair and aristocratic features.

Only eight years Tate's senior, Brit was more of a brother than an uncle. He lived in the carriage house-turned-apartment out back, ran a law office in town, and lived the pleasured life of the consummate bachelor.

His attention drifted over Fiona's head to the brass wall clock. "Someone had better light those candles. Only two minutes to go." Family tradition required they celebrate birthdays at the exact time of arrival.

"I've got it." Sami hurried to the cake and began lighting wicks.

Another streak of lighting lit the front yard with thunder booming almost immediately. The house vibrated.

"Storm's right on top of us," Brit said, frowning at the window as if to fend off the clatter and bang.

"No time to worry about that." Granddad gripped Fiona's shoulders and steered her to the cake. Icing the color of violets glowed beneath twenty-two tiny candles. The sweet scent of vanilla rose with the heat.

Sami rubbed her hands together and glanced at the clock. "See, Tate? All done, and with ten seconds to spare." She waved to Tate, urging her to come closer.

Muscles unbunched in Tate's back as warmth rushed in. There may be wounds waiting for her at home, but her family was the comforting balm.

She edged closer to the table, standing at Fiona's side opposite Sami.

Grandfather led off the birthday song, adding an extra dose of his charming Welsh lilt. When the last refrain fell to silence, Sami whispered to Fiona, "Happy birthday."

Tate touched her shoulder. "Now make a wish."

Fiona's eyes shone like emeralds as she stared into the flames. Hands clasped together, she sucked in a breath that lifted her shoulders.

But before she could blow, lightning cracked across the sky, illuminating the entire kitchen with a blast of white.

Thunder shook the old Victorian frame, rolling through the walls in heavy waves.

Lights flickered throughout. Electricity hummed through the lines and brightened the bulbs to a glare.

Then the house went dark.

2

Fiona blinked rapidly, her face the most visible as she bent toward the burning candles. "I think I'll wait before blowing these out."

"There's a flashlight in the junk drawer." Brit gestured to the counter but jolted when thunder clapped and rumbled around them. Then twice more.

"Three thumps in the house at night." Grandfather tapped his carved wooden cane on the kitchen tile. "Death will follow."

"Dad." Brit shook his head. "I don't think thunder counts."

This wasn't the first time she'd heard her grandfather mention the Welsh superstition, but now the words raised bumps on her arms. Her muscles tightened, held, until air burst from her throat.

Ridiculous, she told herself. She didn't believe in such things.

But when the turbulent weather ceased suddenly, creating a vacuum of silence, she shared a tense moment with her family.

Grandfather held up a hand, a signal to stay still and be quiet.

Expectation welled inside Tate, a creep and tingle up her spine. Premonition.

The jubilant birthday mood was gone, replaced by an inexplicable weight that pulled on the edges of her mind.

She drew a deep breath and would swear the molecules she breathed were abnormally light, almost effervescent. Something had shifted. The atmosphere had changed, had come . . . alive.

A sudden gust swept through the kitchen, extinguishing the

fire in the hearth, as well as the small candles. The force of the unnatural wind blew into Tate's eyes and lifted Sami's hair.

The surge swelled and then collapsed, leaving them in a black void. The only sound was the rain's constant drumming.

"Tate?" Fiona asked with a tremor.

Saying nothing, for she had no explanation, Tate wrapped her arm around her sister's waist. She overlapped Sami's arm, already providing a protective grip on Fiona.

Together the sisters stood, listening, waiting. A faint amber glow appeared near the bay window. The inexplicable light grew until the view of the front yard was obstructed.

In moments, the strange light was brighter than the fire had been, and within its burning center, a figure materialized. A woman, gilded and glittering.

Grandfather grasped the handle of his cane in one hand and curled the fingers of his other around its wooden length. He held the staff in front of his chest in a defensive posture.

"Niall." The woman's amber eyes were afire, shocking against skin dusted with gold. Her voice was warm and rich, yet sweet. Like melted toffee. Yet her tone—bitter. "Would you lift your hand against me? A servant of the *Dea Matrona*?"

Her pursed lips were a mystical shade of gold and rose, befitting her perfectly sculpted face. Her dress draped in folds over one shoulder, the scarlet material startling against her luminous skin.

Grandfather lowered his cane. "No, I . . ." He dropped his head. "Please, forgive my insult."

"The desire to protect your family is no offense." The woman waved a hand of pardon, or dismissal. "The unwise choices you've made in doing so, however . . ."

Grandfather raised his head, met her stare, and took a stumbling step back.

With a shake of her head, the gilded woman turned away from him to scan Tate, Sami, and finally, Fiona. "You are the ones I have come to address."

Tate's tongue felt thick, unable to create coherent language. Who—or *what*—was this woman? She tried to clear her throat and speak.

Sami beat her to it. "Who the hell are you?"

Tate stiffened, but her sister's profanity seemed to amuse rather than offend the woman. "Daughter of Nadia, your bravery pleases me. Yet you will need more than bold words to make use of the opportunity I bring you."

Grasping her head to press against the shock still resonating, Tate forced her voice to work. "Opportunity for what? What is this?"

"Mass delusion." Sami nodded decisively. "Must be a gas leak."

"We don't use gas in this house," Fiona said, her tone soft and filled with awe.

Ignoring their byplay, the woman said, "You need not fear me and may call me Rhiann. I am sent by the Dea Matrona to be her messenger. She has chosen the daughters of Nadia to become *Matronae.*"

While Fiona and Tate both stared, transfixed, Sami took two steps in retreat, held both hands out in front of her chest, and shook her head. "No, no, no. I don't know why we're all seeing this, but I don't want anything more. I don't want to be one of these mat . . . mat . . ."

"Matronae," Brit said, his cadence slow and steady. "The divine mother goddess is a maternal guardian. She is often depicted with sets of three, usually animals or children, examples of those she has assumed care of. They are called Matronae."

Rhiann spoke to their grandfather. "It is good that you have taught your son the old ways, Niall." She tilted her head and studied Brit with an unsettling intensity. "You will require his help before the end."

Tate crossed her arms and glanced back and forth between the two men. How did her uncle know about Matronae? Why were he and Granddad both carrying on a normal conversation as if oddly-colored people popped into the kitchen every day?

Then the messenger's words registered. "The end of what?" Tate asked. "What do you want from us?"

The woman grasped the flowing folds of her crimson dress. "You were dealt a terrible wrong. Unnatural forces have interfered in your lives. Their actions have upset the natural balance."

"What do you mean?" Fiona asked, stepping forward, a countermove to Sami's retreat.

"You lost more than your mother on that night. So much more."

"That's not an answer," Tate said.

Rhiann turned an accusing gaze to their grandfather. "You chose to deny them their birthright. You haven't taught them."

Granddad thrust his cane to the floor with a sharp rap. "You must know why."

"I do, but the reason you denied their training is the very reason they will need it." The laughter from Rhiann was cold and mocking. "Did you believe he would allow such trickery? That he would find another and release you from your debt?"

"Who does she mean? Who do you owe?" Tate studied Granddad, but he only clenched his jaw and offered no reply.

Brit shot a look to Tate and her sisters but refused to make eye contact. His stance was rigid, arms crossed over his chest. He dropped them to his sides, then crossed them again.

Why was he suddenly so nervous? Because of the debt Granddad owed? Or the man who would come to collect?

Tendrils of fear wove their way through her, coils that grew and stretched around her heart, before wrapping into a crushing knot.

The golden Rhiann flung a hand toward Tate and her sisters. "You have precisely three days."

The clock on the wall chimed out, its tiny brass handle striking the bell to begin the count of twelve. "At midnight on the third day, the chance to save yourselves will have passed. You have until then to find the key."

Sami skirted the end of the table, still unwilling to draw close. "What key?"

"Find the key." The woman's burning gaze fell upon Tate. "The key to your happiness."

Then Sami. "The key to your magic."

And Fiona. "To your very lives."

"But—" Tate began, only to be interrupted by the woman.

"The gods have permitted you a small allotment of time to make things right. Dea Matrona has taken up your cause and demanded it be so." She lifted her arm again and pointed over their heads.

Tate turned, as did everyone else.

The terrible lightning and thunder resumed with blasts that flashed inside through the windows and percussion that shook again and again. This time, the strikes kept time with the chiming clock.

On the final bell, the side door of the kitchen flew open. Harsh winds and rain whipped inside. The storm moving in from the Atlantic now raged.

Rhiann began to flicker, to fade, but her pointing finger still aimed toward the back of the house. "Go now. Let her guide you."

As her amber light disappeared, the fireplace erupted with flames.

Sami gripped the edge of the table with both hands. "Tate, what just happened?"

"I have no idea." But she couldn't deny what all five of them had seen and experienced. The woman had been real. And so was the rising storm now rushing inside the house.

There was no way she'd go running out into that mess. Not until she knew more. She faced her grandfather, ready to demand answers.

"Fiona, wait!" Sami yelled.

Tate jerked around to see Fiona rushing toward the open door, her silhouette outlined by flashes of lightning. "Fiona!" Frozen, stunned, Tate stared after her.

"She must not go alone." Still clutching his cane, Granddad hurried toward the open door and invading rain.

Tate and Sami reacted as one and bolted, cutting him off in pursuit of their sister.

"Hurry," Granddad urged from behind. "Go!"

They didn't have to be told again. Outside, rain stung Tate's face and thunder assaulted her ears, but together, she and Sami ran.

3

Tate and Sami raced after Fiona, each step a squish-and-suck as they tramped over the sodden lawn. They rounded the corner of the house in time to see Fiona slow her pace and come to a stop several yards from where the lightning was arcing down to the ground.

Electricity knifed into the earth again and again, striking the exact same spot. Fiona lifted a hand to shield her eyes from the brightness.

Red pines towered at the edge of the lawn, their boughs thrashing in the violent storm. The trees allowed only a partial view of the Atlantic, but through them Tate could see waves rushing toward land. The fast-moving whitecaps told her the sea was in turmoil.

And so was she.

The heavy rain drenched them all, turning Sami's deep auburn curls into thick ropes, while the sheen of Fiona's sleek black reflected the light, shimmering with each strike.

"Fiona, are you crazy?" Sami asked when she came to a standstill beside her younger sister.

Fee shook off Sami's hand when she tried to pull her back to the house. "The messenger said to let her guide us," Fiona said. "Who is *she*? I don't see anyone."

Tate was at a loss. As the eldest, she had always stepped in, taken control, and made sure her sisters were cared for. It pained her to say, "I don't know what to do, Fee."

So the three stood mute, watching the intimidating strikes while rain drummed against their skulls.

Brit arrived next to stand with them, and finally, their grandfather.

Tate swiped water from her face. "I don't understand any of this. What's happening?"

"I'm sorry, Tate," her grandfather said before adding to Sami and Fiona, "I'm so sorry. I thought I could prevent this if I . . ."

"What? Tell me," Tate croaked, her throat squeezing in on itself. The man she trusted most in the world had clearly kept great secrets from them. And what of Brit?

Tate faced her uncle, but he held up a hand. "There's no time to explain now. All you can do is follow your instincts." He gestured to the lightning as it continued to spear into the dark earth. "This is for the three of you."

"Yes," her grandfather said. "If you feel an impulse, you must act on it."

"Impulse?" Sami threw out her hands. "My impulse is to get back inside the house like any sane person." She shook Fiona's shoulder. "We need to go back."

"No." Fiona responded by grabbing Sami's hand and then Tate's, linking the three of them. "We can't be afraid."

The blinding collision of sky to earth was relentless, and the noise—the brain-crushing noise!

Tate pivoted to stare directly into the streaks of light as if an answer would appear. A tiny part of her screamed with recognition. An unbidden urge pushed her to move, to act.

With rainwater streaming over her cheeks, she released her sister's hand and moved toward the lightning in slow but determined steps. She heard Sami say her name but didn't look back.

Fiona was right. They couldn't be afraid.

She and her sisters had been directed here. Their grandfather believed Rhiann had been sent by a goddess. He had absolute faith.

And despite the fantastic truths he'd kept hidden, Tate trusted her grandfather.

She eased around to the far side of the epicenter, now blackened and charred from the continuous onslaught. She held out her hands. And felt nothing.

No heat, no sizzle of energy. The incredible bursts and accompanying sounds were real, but nothing else. She sniffed. No scent of ozone, only the rain.

Had the lightning been sent by the goddess? The Dea Matrona?

Sami and Fiona followed her lead, taking up positions around the black hole in the ground that deepened with every spear of light. Tate might not feel heat, but the strikes contained enough force to pummel the grass and dirt.

As soon as they were at equal distances around the pit, the lightning struck one final time with a mighty clap. Sound waves blasted raindrops outward to slap and sting Tate's skin.

She stared at the caved-in ground, her breath heaving in and out as she waited for whatever came next. The earth was scorched, demarcated by a jagged black line, even as water continued to pour from the sky.

What could burn the grass without heat?

A word came to her mind, but she shook it away.

She fixed her gaze on the darkened earth, and then, as she watched, the soil in the very center of the pit moved. She squinted, wiped her plastered hair from her eyes. Large drops hitting the dirt?

No. The disturbance was coming from below the surface. Something was pushing outward, from beneath.

Tate sucked in a breath. She and her sisters circled around. But what was rising from the earth?

A warning built in her throat, an urge to tell her sisters to run.

Sami gaped. "Guys, maybe we should—"

A tiny bud of gold popped its head from the wet soil.

Fiona lifted a halting hand to Sami. "Wait. What is that?"

Tate kept her eyes locked on the small shoot as it unfolded. The nodule was lengthening, growing. But too quickly, like a sprout filmed at natural speed then played back a hundred times faster.

Soon the seedling reached the height of her knees, still sparkling gold on the surface but with a ruby hue flowing inside. What kept this thing alive? What made it grow so quickly?

Tate's heart stuttered, and her mind tripped over that word again.

Fiona exhaled and finally said it. "It's magic."

The stalk was up to the level of their hips when three points sprouted and unfurled into stems. Curling and waving, they undulated through the rain.

Another bud formed on top of the stalk, rounding, expanding, and finally, opening. A flower blossomed, replete with golden sepals to protect the young crimson bloom.

"It's beautiful," Fiona said with wonder. "I don't know what we did, or what someone else did, for us to be so lucky."

"Lucky?" Sami scoffed, shoving wet hair back from her face. "We don't know what this thing is, Fee. So stay back."

"It won't hurt us." Fiona's gaze was riveted to the spreading petals. She swayed. "How could it? It's so beautiful. So . . . beautiful."

Fiona seemed dazed, intoxicated. She stared at the bloom as if in worship.

"Fiona?" Sami said.

Fiona leaned forward, toward the flower and its seeking limbs. *The flower.*

Tate's chest clutched. "Fiona, stop looking at it!"

As if they knew their ploy had failed, the stems lashed out to capture each of their wrists.

Sami yelped and used her free hand to scratch at the vine encasing her arm.

Tate tried to jerk free as the limb curled up and around her forearm. There was no pain, but the vine constricted, securing its hold.

Even Fiona snapped out of her stupor and began struggling, but her feet slipped each time she tried to gain purchase on the soggy ground.

The enchanting bloom had been a ruse. It's golden limbs were shackles, meant to ensnare the three who'd summoned it.

Tate slid on the wet lawn as the plant pulled her in. Digging in her heels, Tate looked to see the same panic flare to life in Sami and contort her face.

Brit lunged to intervene but Granddad held him back. "Wait. Just wait."

With a roll of crimson through its base, the plant gave a forceful yank, trying to reel in its vines and the prey it had captured.

"No!" Fiona shrieked.

A stream of invective flowed from Sami's mouth.

Brit leaned forward with his fists clenched, but he was still held in check by his father's hand in the center of his chest.

Tate's stare clashed with her grandfather's as she lowered her center of gravity and leaned backward. She and her sisters were losing the tug of war.

Why had they been sent out here? Was it a trap?

An empowering mix of anger and denial rolled through her, and like the pulsing red within the plant, she envisioned her own strength surging.

"Pull together!" she shouted to Sami and Fiona. "Together!"

Sami nodded and paused. She timed her next tug with Tate's, but Fiona slipped and landed on her backside. Tate and Sami pulled again, grunting with the exertion.

With a short scream of frustration, Fiona scrambled back to her feet and threw her weight into the next tug, just as her sisters timed theirs again.

A ripping sound split the air as the plant lurched forward, exposing the top of its roots. They had wrenched it partially from the soil.

"Again!" Sami yelled, and the three of them jerked their arms with renewed determination.

Another shredding sound as dark red roots were disinterred, flapping and wiggling.

As it broke free from the earth, its blossom split into three parts. Then the entire thing erupted into crimson and gold sparks.

The brilliant particles lifted on the wind and scattered over the ground. They settled on the darkened grass and dirt like unearthed treasure.

The rain began to slow, turning to a mild shower.

"Yes!" Grandfather yelled, thrusting his cane into the air.

Fiona crumpled to the ground, and Sami bent over, hands on her knees, both of them panting with fatigue.

Tate ran a hand down her muddy clothing. Her entire body hummed as shock, terror, and adrenaline overwhelmed her system. She dropped in a heap, unmindful of the mud oozing through her fingers and beneath her legs.

Exhausted, yes. Frightened, definitely.

But a sense of triumph filled her and had a laugh fluttering for release. She felt as if she'd won a contest or passed an important test.

Sami, still resting with her hands on her knees, jutted her chin to indicate the pit. "What is that?"

Fiona rolled to her knees to look. Her voice was higher pitched, excited. "Something's in there."

"Great. What next?" Tate dared a peek into the hole.

When Sami glanced over, Tate gave her a shrug-nod combo. They all crept closer for a better look.

Sami reached down to scrape away mud and caked-on dirt from some kind of metal container. She gripped the sides, dragging a box-shaped object to the grass.

Her fingers worked with the rain to clear away soil, revealing a silver chest, approximately eighteen inches square. "The design is simple, no markings." Sami ran a finger across the front. "It's been soldered shut."

"She will guide you." In a somber tone, their grandfather repeated the messenger's words.

"Who?" Tate clambered to stand. She pressed the middle finger of each hand to her thumbs.

She pressed harder and asked the question burning in her brain, in her heart. The one she already knew the answer to. "Who left this here?"

Granddad continued to regard the silver box. Though rain still trickled down their faces, he wiped suspiciously at his cheek. "Your mother."

4

Sami released her hold on the chest and sat back in the grass. "Mom left this here?" Her voice was flat.

Brit kneeled beside her. He scanned the yard before hefting the metal box. "Let's move inside."

"Why would she bury a chest?" Fiona asked, trailing after her uncle while Sami and Tate remained motionless, still shell-shocked.

Tate's fingers hurt from driving into her thumbs, so she released the pressure and let out a breath. Her heartbeat slowed as the storm quelled, and in the softening drizzle, she crossed to Sami, extending a hand to help her up.

"Why is this happening, Tate?" Sami slung her hands to disperse the clinging mud.

Shaking her head, Tate looked to her grandfather who waited for them. "I don't know." She met Sami's stare, swore a silent oath. "But we're going to find out."

The wind struck their backs, colder and more insistent.

"Yeah we are, because I don't like any of this." Sami started to move, then stilled to whisper, "What was she hiding? Why bury a box in the ground?"

As Tate readied her reply, she saw fog creeping from the surrounding woods as the bay of some hellish creature echoed from the forest.

Granddad stopped walking. He scoured the dark expanse of the yard as mist licked over the grass, crawling closer.

He leapt in front of them with unexpected agility. "Get behind me."

The fog engulfed them, a tendril of mist curling up and around Tate's leg. Cold spiked in her calf, so she jerked from its grasp.

Another howl and her heart rate ratcheted up. She scanned the tree line, searching for the source of the awful cry.

Red eyes, bright against the black, emerged just before a hound appeared. This was no normal dog, it's oversized body dark but misted with a crimson haze. The square snout held powerful-looking jaws, and the rumble Tate heard was the beast's low, menacing growl.

The teeth snapped together as the creature homed in on Tate and Sami.

Suddenly the atmosphere began to blush, the pale light on Sami's face growing pink. Tate looked up to the sky, and even through the quicksilver clouds, through her own disbelief, she saw.

Blood on the moon.

"Brit!" her grandfather barked, still on guard.

Brit dropped the chest, raised his empty hands. "I've got nothing."

"Then go!"

Brit turned his head, and then bolted across the yard to his apartment in the carriage house.

With slow, cautious steps, Granddad edged back, keeping Tate and Sami behind him. Another howl rang out, and he cursed when the beast was joined by two . . . no, three more of its kind.

Tate felt sick with fear, light in the head. But when Sami made a soft, mewling sound in her throat, something snapped inside Tate and brought the world into crystalline focus. She couldn't just stand here and do nothing.

"Forget the box," she called to Fiona, who was trying to drag the metal chest. Taking Sami's hand to pull her along, Tate rushed to catch up to their sister. "We need to move."

"Tate!" Granddad yelled.

The urgency in his cry made her whip around to see that the first hound had given chase.

With a cry of alarm, she pushed closer to her sisters, but the beast ran in a wide arc, cutting off their escape. Snapping and snarling, spittle the color of blood flying from its mouth, the great dog corralled them back toward their grandfather.

The dog's head was the size of a cement block with bear-trap jaws. One bite would destroy their flesh, crush their bones to pulp. Tate shuddered as nausea rolled up from her gut.

"Don't move!" her grandfather shouted again, rage and terror battling in his voice. He eased closer to where the three of them stood huddled together. "Stay very still, girls. You aren't equipped for this."

How could anyone be equipped? They looked like dogs from Hell.

"No sudden movements," Granddad warned. He angled to stand between his granddaughters and the beasts come to hunt them.

"What do they want with us?" Fiona sounded close to tears.

Granddad sent them a sidelong glance. "Just stay where you are." With one hand he gripped the silver handle of his cane, the other its wooden shaft. In one quick motion, he stripped away the sheath to reveal a long, thin sword.

Sami gasped. "Granddad!"

Tate silently agreed. *Who is this man?* His blue eyes, so normally tender, were now ablaze with . . . ferocity.

He slashed the sword through the air so it whistled. "Come on, ye' bloody mongrels."

Eyeing the blade, the four hulking dogs took measured steps to form a perimeter around their small group. They moved in sync, as if they had a plan.

"Damn you," Granddad uttered, his hard gaze flitting between the hounds as they closed in.

Tate whirled to face outward on the opposite side, keeping Sami and Fiona in the middle. Her nerves sang, and her skin shivered as she waited for one of the monsters to pounce.

One of the hounds yelped and reared up on its hind legs, front paws kicking the air as it growled and whined. Then another sharp cry when a silver point erupted from its chest.

The hound jolted, went still, and crumpled to the ground.

Behind the beast stood Brit, panting and rain-drenched . . . with a crossbow in his arms.

And Tate's mind peeled back yet another layer from a family she no longer recognized.

The fallen beast dissolved into a sizzling liquid, boiling blood seeping into waterlogged soil. Those that remained raised their heads to bay at the scarlet moon.

One of the hounds broke into a run and barreled at Granddad. Although he was ready and struck out with the sword, he missed the creature by inches when it leapt over his head.

The hellish hound wasn't interested in their grandfather. Its ravenous eyes sought only Tate and her sisters.

"No!" Tate jumped in front of Sami and Fiona and flung her arms wide. The beast landed, then pushed off its haunches to lunge for her throat.

Another well-aimed bolt skewered the dog's ribs to send it spiraling sideways. With no sound at all, the thing quickly bled to a puddle like its brethren before.

Tate watched as the light rain pattered into the pool, creating a macabre watercolor of blood and muck.

With the second hound's death, the remaining two fell into a frenzy, both snarling and snapping as they rushed the women.

Granddad headed one off while Brit fired on the other, but this time, the beast reacted, lurching forward and hunching down. The bolt sailed over its back.

Tate heard Brit curse as he reloaded. She whirled left and right, trying to keep an eye on both threats.

A force inside whispered to her, urging her to act, to defend! But she didn't recognize this secret warrior. She had no idea what it wanted her to do.

Both hounds were close now, but Granddad could only take one. He lifted his sword, prepared this time when the beast tried to jump. He waited, timed his strike perfectly, and cleanly beheaded the hound on its upward leap.

"Dad!" Brit yelled. "I can't risk a shot!" The last dog had crept in close, crowding them. If Brit's aim was off, he might hit one of his family.

The hound had slowed but was only a few feet away. Tate pressed against Sami and Fee.

The dog suddenly stopped, perked its ears. Then with a grunt, it raced in the direction of the forest.

Female laughter echoed from the sky and made the red pines tremble. The sound doubled upon itself, again and again, until it seemed a hundred hags cackled in the crimson night.

But no woman appeared.

"Who . . ." Granddad started. "Do you see anything?"

"No, " Sami and Tate both said.

It was Brit who shouted, "More!" and pointed toward the trees.

Three new hounds had come to join the fray. They lined up with the other beast, lowered their heads, and charged.

Brit immediately took one down, but he was still yards away.

Granddad turned to fend off another and slipped in the mud.

So neither man was there when the first dog rammed into Tate and knocked her to the ground. She landed hard, twisting her hand so that pain streaked up her wrist.

Sami screamed when another dog crashed into her. The hit sent her flying.

Tate rolled over, cradling her arm. She and Sami were both on the ground when the hounds turned. They were too far away when the beasts circled back.

And when they went for Fiona, who now stood alone.

"Fee!" Tate cried out, trying to get to her feet. But by the time she was up, the creatures were surrounding their prey.

Fiona's frightened eyes met Tate's. Her mouth fell open as if to cry out.

The hounds rushed, and she went down.

"Fee!" Sami threw herself toward the dogs but fell short, her fingers grasping at empty air.

One hound latched sharp teeth onto the hem of Fiona's blue jeans while another came in from her opposite side. The second clamped its massive jaws onto Fiona's ankle.

Her scream of pain ripped through the air, and tore into Tate.

The dogs bulleted away, dragging Fiona with them. She bumped over the ground as they hauled her toward the forest.

Toward the cliffs.

Terror chased the breath from Tate's body, so she couldn't scream, couldn't speak. She scrambled to her feet, stumbled, slipped, and finally gained traction to sprint after her sister.

Her heart was choking her, and she couldn't suck in enough air. But she kept running, pumping her legs as hard and fast as she could.

A long, keening howl told her Brit or Granddad had killed another dog, but she focused ahead, on Fiona's stark white face.

Footsteps pounded into the mucky ground behind her. "Hurry, Tate!" Sami was coming up quick, her longer legs eating up the distance. She passed Tate to burst from the trees seconds before her.

The hounds had taken Fiona to the edge of the cliffs but had released her to bay at the murder-red moon.

Sami sprung from a full-sprint, landing close enough to grab

Fiona's outstretched hands. "Hold on, Fee! Hold on to me!"

Fiona's mouth was wide but soundless. Still, she managed to clamp her fingers onto Sami's.

The hound that had bitten Fiona chomped down on her leg again and jerked its head to pull her farther. Fiona's body slid easily on the damp earth, and soon her feet dangled over the side as pebbles and soil gave way.

Tate fell to the ground beside Sami, heedless of the hounds that could turn at any moment and rip them to pieces. "We've got you," she told Fiona, the words rushing out between her heavy breaths.

"Let her go!" Sami started kicking the dog nearest her, drawing its attention.

The hound dropped Fiona's leg and turned on Sami, massive jaws wide as it growled in her face.

"No, no," Tate pleaded. She couldn't hold Fee and help Sami too.

The bloody jaws drew closer, and Sami clenched her eyes shut. She whimpered, "Tate."

"Be gone!" An authoritative voice resonated through the darkness.

Both hounds ceased movement and stopped snarling. The one pulling at Fiona's pants lowered to its belly with a whimper. Its partner did the same.

Both bowed their massive heads in submission, gave mournful howls, and vanished.

Released at last, Fiona started to cry as Sami and Tate crawled to her, taking her in their arms.

"Oh my God, Fee. Are you okay?" Tate wrapped an arm around Fiona's back and then hauled Sami into an awkward hug, grateful they were all alive.

Her chest and throat still felt too crowded, her lungs burned, and it took a few seconds for the white noise of panic to subside. Finally, she remembered they weren't alone.

She pulled away from her sisters to find a strange man looking down on them. He wore all black beneath a vest the color of midnight smoke. No, not just a vest. Tate recognized the garment as a doublet.

With the disappearance of the hounds, the moon had returned to its usual white. The gentle illumination gleamed on the stranger's ebony hair, chiseling his features with night's shadow.

Tate could only gawk, for there were no words.

His beauty shot through her like arrows of light.

"I despise bloodhounds." Steepling his fingers, he lowered onyx eyes to the women on the ground. "Which is likely the reason *she* so adores them."

"Who?" Tate heard herself say, though the sound seemed distant and not her own.

The man dropped to one knee and reached for Fiona. Sami reacted, leaning over to shield her sister, but the stranger simply moved her arm aside.

He put two fingers to Fiona's thigh.

"What are you doing?" Sami demanded.

Fiona's breath escaped like wind through a straw. Her brows winged upward. "Oh." She relaxed into a smile.

Before Tate could question her, the stranger shifted and touched her injured wrist with the same two fingers. She'd managed to ignore the burning sensation, but now he erased the pain with a gentle stroke.

With the ache gone and the danger removed, her mind began to crowd with questions.

A deity's messenger had crashed Fiona's birthday party, Brit and Granddad were closet warriors, dogs made of blood, and now a total stranger who healed with his fingertips.

He cocked a haughty brow and smiled as if he knew a secret.

Tate had had enough. Keeping a hand on Fiona, she stood. "Thank you for . . . whatever you just did, but we have to go. It's not safe out here."

"Agreed." Sami tried to rise but faltered, unsure of what to do when the man held out his hand to her.

"Please don't thank me." His words were terse. "I mean that."

Finally he took Sami's hand for himself and pulled her up. Then he eased in close—too close—using the same hand to brush mud from her cheek. "My dear Samantha. I must say, you are breathtaking. Even more so in person."

Tate's skin prickled. This man had banished the hounds and healed their injuries, but his words were too precise, his stare too greedy. Everything about him made her instincts scream.

Ulterior motives slithered beneath the charm.

She would have stepped between the man and Sami, but Granddad and Brit burst from the woods.

Granddad assessed Tate, Sami, and Fiona, one by one. "You're safe," he rasped, before closing his eyes in what seemed to be a silent prayer of thanks.

When he opened them again, the fierceness Tate had noticed before blazed to life once again. But this time, his hateful gaze was aimed at the dark-haired man.

Granddad's blue eyes narrowed and his upper lip curled. He made a strange, chuffing sound in his throat, and said, "Emuirdane."

5

"I see I arrived just in time." The stranger, Emuirdane, dusted his hands together as he faced the men.

"You set those hounds on my girls." Granddad took a threatening step forward.

Emuirdane lifted a hand. "Stop. Consider the error of your assumption." He spread his arms in a gallant gesture that ill-befitted the sly tone of his voice. "Would I ever hurt them? The three who shall deliver my greatest desire?

"No," he answered himself, sending a cunning look to Tate and her sisters. "Those blood-drenched creatures belong to Hellana."

"What?" Granddad narrowed his eyes. "Who is—"

"That is a long and complicated story," Emuirdane said, returning the glare Granddad threw him. "Besides, I'd much rather share a different tale. One of a young man, voyaging to the New World with his lovely and gifted young bride."

"No." Granddad lifted his sword to point at Emuirdane. "Why are you here?"

"To be of assistance. I came to the aid of your granddaughters, and even saved the life of your youngest." He tossed a careless hand to Tate and her sisters. "Ask them."

Tate nodded, but with hesitation. "It's true."

"This man gives nothing for free." Brit moved, aligning himself with his nieces. "Answer my father, Emuirdane. Why have you come?"

"These three have a quest before them. They will face peril and doubt along the way." The raven-haired man smiled, but its warmth didn't reach his eyes. "You may consider me . . . their protector."

Brit slung his bow over his shoulder. "They don't need your protection."

"I would differ, considering young Fiona is alive and standing on two feet instead of one." His expression turned to stone as disdain slipped through his slick exterior. "Thanks only to me."

Rescuer or not, Tate was ready to be free of Emuirdane's presence. So she opted for a neutral route. "Yes, and I think we should get Fiona inside and take a look at that ankle."

He bowed his head. "Of course." But when Tate shifted, the man raised a finger to hold her in place. "But your arm. How does it feel, Tate?"

"Better. I'm grateful." Her supposed gratitude sounded stiff, but the most primitive part of her brain buzzed a low yet insistent warning. This man was dangerous, frightening her in a way the hounds had not.

He stepped in front of her, intentionally blocking her view of her grandfather. "Before you go, I must be sure you know." He touched her wrist, reminding her of what he'd done. "You have powers of your own."

Tate pulled her hand back. "Excuse me?"

"Others have unfairly denied you these gifts." He waved a hand to encompass her sisters. "But now the three of you must find your way to the source. If you don't, you *will* fail."

"Why do you want to be our protector?" Fiona asked. "Why do you care?"

"I'm here to help you, never doubt. But I have also come for reasons of my own." Emuirdane put a hand to his chest and curled his fingers as if trying to hold something that wasn't there. "Something precious of mine has been . . . lost. I believe it is nearby."

His stance changed to one of aggression as he turned to Granddad. "There is also the matter of promises made and debts to be paid."

Alarm bells went off in Tate's mind. This was the man Rhiann had been talking about. The man their grandfather was indebted to.

Too many strange pieces. And none of them fitting together.

"No more." Granddad pushed past Emuirdane to stand with Brit, creating a male barrier between the stranger and his granddaughters. "You have no right."

Tate blinked as she looked over Brit's shoulder. Emuirdane's visage had morphed. Though almost undetectable, she swore the cavities of his eyes deepened, his jaw grew more pronounced.

"I have every right!" Chunks of dirt crumbled from the cliffs as Emuirdane's anger roared past them and out over the Atlantic.

A ring on his hand began to glow, the large stone center whirling an oily blackish-green. "You have wasted time, old man. You've put them at risk with your foolishness, and I'll not stand by any longer."

Brit met the stranger's indignation with his own. "Then tell us who threatens them. Who is Hellana?"

Emuirdane didn't answer him but stroked his palms down the front of his gray doublet. And with the caress he changed again, regained his composure. In a more subdued manner, he addressed Sami directly. "You and your sisters are helpless without the truth, and I can no longer tolerate this deception."

"I will tell them everything. Tonight." Granddad hissed air through his teeth, like someone had just poked an open wound. "I know my mistake, and the goddess has made her wishes clear."

"Goddess?" Emuirdane cocked one side of his mouth into a mocking grin. "Tell me, truly, do you cower before this obscure deity? One whom you have never seen?"

He rubbed his ring. "Or should you fear he who stands before you?"

Apparently pleased by Granddad's silence, he released a harsh laugh before turning to the sisters. He crossed one hand over his stomach, one behind his back and bowed to them.

Then he walked around them and off the edge of the cliff.

Tate held her breath, sure he would fall. But a network of dark threads spread before him. High above the rocks and sea, the magical walkway knit itself into existence and caught his every step.

Tate and her family watched his departure.

Until Emuirdane was swallowed by a mist of silver clouds.

~~~

Tate and Fiona were the first ones to gather in the kitchen after showering and changing clothes. Though to be fair, Sami and Brit had detoured beforehand and gone for tools to open the chest.

Unchanged since her death, their mother's workshop still stood in back, an offshoot of the carriage house where their uncle lived. The room held everything she'd used for metal work, likely the same tools she'd used to create the chest.

Tate rubbed her chilled fingers together as she studied the small circular saw sitting next to the mystery box they'd pulled from the ground.

Fiona stood at the kitchen counter, her arms hanging limply at her side and her pale face absent its usual peace. Before she'd been excited by the concept of magic, and the existence of gods and fairy folk.

But now her mouth was tight as she stared at the glass-paned cabinets. "I'll make some coffee." She lifted a hand, paused, and then pivoted to the other counter. "Or maybe hot chocolate. It's so late."

The attack on her body, on her life, had taken their toll. The previous fantasy of goddesses and golden ladies had been cast in a gruesome new light.

"I'll help you make decaf," Brit said as he entered. His dark hair was still damp, dripping on the shoulders of his Yale-blue T-shirt. The exact shade of his troubled eyes.

Tate wondered anew about his choice to stay in Bar Harbor, to live on the family property. Had the secret life he'd known of swayed his decisions? Had he stayed here to watch over Sami and Fee?

When she had run as fast and as far as she could?

Granddad and Sami could be heard talking as they came down the stairs, so she chose not to dwell on questions she'd have answers to soon enough.

Sami sniffed the air. "Hmm, coffee. My saviors," she said as she headed over to wait for the pot to fill. Her attempt at levity was the only crack in the impenetrable tension weighing them down.

Fiona broke the heavy silence. "I've been wondering. If Mom left that box there, then what about the flower? Why did it attack us?"

"Attack?" Brit leaned against the counter. "Or simply force you to respond? The flower didn't hurt you, did it?"

"Well, no."

"Your mother left the box, and I believe she enchanted it. So only you three could raise it from the ground. And only," he wagged a finger, "if you did it together."

"What do you mean Mom enchanted the box?" Sami asked. "What are you saying?"

Tate and Fiona shared a glance, neither as stunned by Brit's choice of words as they would have been even a few hours earlier.

But Sami was still doing her best to stay entrenched in denial. No one answered her question, but she fell silent and didn't ask gain.

Several strained minutes later, the coffee was ready. Brit poured a cup and walked over to the metal box. He stared as the fire's reflection burnished the silver. "I have to be honest. I'm relieved we can finally stop hiding the truth from you."

Sami put her hands together, cracked her knuckles. "I can't believe you two have known about all this," she waved a hand in a circle, "this *crazy shit*, and never told us. You've lied to us our whole lives."

"We didn't always," Brit said. "We didn't decide until—"

"Brit." Granddad shook his head. "Let me. This is my responsibility."

Brit inclined his head, deferring to his father.

Granddad took a seat, rested his threaded fingers on the table, and sighed as he searched for where to begin. "You know your grandmother and I came from different backgrounds. She was Romanian. I was from Wales. We loved each other very much, had two beautiful children."

Granddad glanced to his son. "That's the short and simple version. What you don't know, is what our families had in common. You weren't brought up as I was, as Brit was." His brow drooped. "As your mother was."

He coughed, took a drink, and clarified, "Both our lineages, our histories, were steeped in magick."

Fiona shifted her weight from one hip to another. "Not the magic as in abracadabra?"

"No, no." He pressed his middle finger into his thumb—a move Tate had stolen from him—and shook his hand as he enunciated, *"Magick,"* with a hard *kuh* at the end. "Arcane energy, hidden currents that flow throughout our world."

Here he licked his lips. "And others."

"Other worlds?" Fiona's interest peaked.

Grandfather gave a solemn nod, not nearly as pleased with this fact as Fiona seemed to be.

"But," he said, returning to his lecture, "only certain people can tap into these mystical currents. No one really knows why. Sometimes the gift skips a child or even generations before reappearing. Your grandmother and I both came from such bloodlines."

Smiling a sad, nostalgic smile, he added, "Though she was much more talented than I."

Granddad pointed to Brit. "Your uncle has his own gifts, like me. But your mother . . ." He gripped his hands together, studied his fingers. "My Nadia. She was the first in our families to have such power."

He gestured to Tate, then Sami and Fiona. "She passed her skill on to you girls."

Fiona continued to stand silently, listening with her delicate features set into an expression of curiosity. Tate absorbed and processed what she could.

But Sami chuckled. "You're kidding, right? I can't do anything special. I don't have any magick. Never have."

"You did," Brit interjected. "When you were young. We agreed not to encourage you, because we didn't want your powers to develop."

"Why didn't you want us to have the magick?" Fiona asked.

"It was my decision," Granddad said. "I thought I was protecting you."

Tate opened her mouth, but her grandfather held his palm up. His sigh was long and weary, expelling twenty years' worth of pent-up secrets. "The first time I met Emuirdane was on the boat carrying your grandmother and me to this country. I thought him just another passenger, a fellow traveler, so we talked. We shared details."

"But all Emuirdane shared was a lie," Brit said, crossing his arms. "Everything he says or does is misdirection or manipulation. You must remember that."

Fiona nodded. "I promise."

Why was she taking this all in so readily—almost eagerly? Sami was skeptical, even after all they'd seen, but Tate just listened, forcing herself to accept the situation, however unbelievable.

"Your grandmother saw Emuirdane for what he was the moment she laid eyes on him. She pulled me away, told me he was *Iele*."

"I've never heard of that," Sami said.

"No, you wouldn't have, would you?" Granddad went on. "The Romanians respect and fear the Iele. They're known to be magical creatures, similar to the Fae my own people believe in. Your grandmother recognized his status by the fibula he wore to hold his cloak together."

"A fibula?" Tate asked, feeling the first hint of intrigue.

"Like a large pin or brooch, only much larger and more decorative. Emuirdane's was silver, the front plate covered by green gems." His brows clashed together. "He wasn't wearing it tonight. Perhaps that is what he wants you to find for him."

"Yes," Fiona put her hands together. "He said he wouldn't harm us, because we would be the ones to give him . . ."

"His greatest desire," Tate finished.

Granddad's eyes lifted up and to the right as he remembered. "I thought the gems were emeralds, but your grandmother said they were not of our world. Instead, enchanted stones worn only by Iele royalty. She could see the unnatural light they gave off, but I could not."

"Sounds like something Emuirdane wouldn't want to lose."

Granddad nodded to Tate. "I didn't see the dark stranger again until the following year." With a sigh, he stared into the darkness that lay beyond the fire's yellow light. "Your mother was just an infant, so young. And she was sick. The doctors gave us no hope."

Two of those misfit pieces clicked together for Tate. "But he gave you that hope, didn't he? Emuirdane."

"Yes." Granddad rubbed a hand over his eyes. "He promised me my daughter would live. My tiny baby. But first, I had to swear an oath. He said my blood was special, and that one day he would require assistance."

Granddad pounded a fist on the table. "But he spoke in riddles. He misled me with double-speak. Nadia, and you girls. *You* are my blood, and that is what he meant. Your mother inherited two different but very strong types of magick, and she then passed it on to you."

He reached out and took Tate's hand. "When I made the bargain, I didn't know. I didn't understand." He shook his head, eyes watering. "But what could I have done? My little girl was dying."

Tate went to her grandfather, the man who'd raised her, cared for her, a man who'd been given an impossible choice. She kneeled beside him just as Sami and Fiona closed in.

"You did what you had to do," Tate said. "You saved Mom, and by saving her, you allowed us be born. We wouldn't even be here without you."

"But now you are the ones who must fulfill my promise. Without your mother . . ."

Sami bent to hug him, and Fiona kissed his cheek, took his cup to refill it.

"No sense in second-guessing, Granddad." Tate used a calm but firm tone. In the face of emotion, she would use logic. "Any of us would have done the same."

"Perhaps."

"You saved Mom and then tried to save us as well by denying us our magick." Tate nodded, to herself as much as him. "You thought Emuirdane couldn't use us if we didn't have any power."

"Yes. I hoped he would forget you." Granddad closed his eyes. "I prayed."

Fiona returned with a steaming cup. Granddad thanked her quietly. And said nothing more.

After a moment, and with Granddad still visibly upset, Brit took over the telling. "Nothing happened again, not for years.

Nadia grew into an adult. She met your father and had all of you.

"But before her death, she began acting strangely. Of course she was grieving for your father, after the cancer . . ." Brit cleared his throat. "Then months later, she went to Dad, shaken and pale. She asked for our mother's grimoire."

"A grimoire?" Tate had a flash of her grandmother and a large green book. "What happened to it?"

"We never saw it again," Brit said. "After your mother got the book, she locked herself inside her workshop for almost two days. She didn't come out, not for food or drink. I'm not sure she even slept."

Granddad spoke abruptly. "I should have known. I should have done *something*."

"Dad, don't." Brit's features grew stern. "We had no way to know what she was planning." He held out his hands to Tate and her sisters. "We hardly saw her the last day she was alive, and for all we know, we couldn't have stopped her if we'd tried."

Brit looked to the side, and Tate knew he was imagining the cliffs. "I have to believe she died for a reason. The grimoire, her behavior. She had to have been working strong magick."

He made a sound of disgust. "The sister I knew would never have killed herself and left you girls without *very* good reason. I believe she used her own death to strengthen the spell."

Sami shoved a hand into her thick auburn hair. "What spell? What could have been important enough to die for?"

"You said she was upset." Fiona touched her lips, fingers shaking. "Maybe something scared her."

"Then why didn't she tell Granddad and Brit?" Sami held out her hands. "They could have helped her."

"No," Tate said. "They would have stopped her. And she couldn't allow that."

"Why not?" Fiona asked.

"There's only one reason she would have taken her life." Tate felt the cold winds of the coming winter blow through her. "To protect us."

Granddad and Brit were silent. Fiona's solemn eyes moistened as she looked at Tate.

But Sami slapped her palms together and strode toward the fireplace. "I don't want to believe that. I don't want to believe any of this."

"We have to deal with this, Sami," Tate said.

"I know that. I know!" Both hands curled into fists, she let her head fall forward. "But I need the truth."

"There's only one way we might find an answer."

Sami was already way ahead of her. She kneeled by the hearth and picked up the saw. "We have to open this box."

6

Sami angled the saw like the professional she was. With a skilled hand, she cut a line around the top of the box, overpowering the room with the grating whine of spinning blade on steel.

The kitchen wasn't an ideal place for such a job, but with bloodhounds stalking the night—hunting for Whiteburn females—they'd all agreed to remain indoors.

Fiona watched with laser-like intensity, fidgeting her hands by alternately rubbing them together and then up and down the fronts of her thighs. She'd been dragged over harsh terrain toward a fall that would have crashed her fragile body to rocks and sea far below, yet here she was, practically standing on her toes with anticipation.

Tate studied the baby sister she and Sami had always felt indebted to not only cherish, but also protect. Maybe little Fee wasn't as fragile as they thought.

Still with a controlled grip on the saw, Sami ended the cut exactly where she'd started. With the division complete, the top of the box shifted to one side.

Tate caught herself holding her breath, saw Fiona doing the same. Then they both exhaled when Sami whisked away the lid.

"This isn't as ornate as Mom's usual work," Sami said, "but still, I hate to destroy it."

Tate and Fiona both inched closer, but Brit and Granddad stayed back, silently acknowledging that this discovery was meant for the girls.

Tate touched Sami's shoulder, notched her chin toward the open chest, giving her the go-ahead. Sami reached in and pulled out a small burlap sack.

Once done, she stepped away to allow her sisters the same opportunity. Tate appreciated the gesture, but she wanted Fiona to go next. "It's for all of us, Fee."

They had no idea how many articles were inside the chest, but Fiona had missed out on so much already. Tate would make sure she wasn't left out of this precious moment.

Fiona grasped a larger object, wrapped in burlap and shaped like a book. With reverent hands, she held it in front of her and moved aside.

Tate edged up to the hearth and stared down into the box. Her heart twisted painfully to find it empty. The child in her yearned for both parents, and though they had passed long ago, the memory of her mother persisted.

She swore, even now, she could still smell the lemon and rose oil her mother had often rubbed on her wrists. Her presence surrounded Tate, her loving lullaby-voice still echoed.

The familiar sadness was sharp and swift as she realized she wouldn't receive a final gift from the mother she missed so much.

Without a sound, Brit drew close and wrapped an arm around her. Still supporting her, he leaned in to examine the box. Then he nudged her arm and pointed to the front corner. "Look."

Tate peered inside. There, standing upright against the side and previously hidden from sight, was an envelope. A small creamy square cloaked in shadow.

Tate picked it up and instinctually closed her eyes, taking in the paper's subtle fragrance. She hadn't been imaging things after all. The envelope bore the barest trace of lemon and rose.

The paper had stood on edge only because it was stuck in a slit at the bottom. Scrutinizing the slight gap, she realized a metal panel spanned the length and width of the chest, secured by notches in the interior.

"There's more." She slid a fingernail beneath one corner and removed the divider.

The others crowded around as she retrieved a box of rich cherry-toned wood from the very bottom of the chest. The wood gleamed, a curve of golden light flashing over the lid, despite having been buried for so long.

"I know that box," Granddad said. He rolled his lips inward in thought, nodding to himself. "What will you open first?"

Tate put the wooden box on the table and looked to her sisters. "Together?"

Fiona and Sami nodded, and as one, they opened the individual items they'd chosen.

Sami pulled out a locket from the small sack, while Fiona unwrapped what was indeed a book. The cover—just as Tate remembered it—was aged green leather with a pattern embossed in gold.

The grimoire.

After a pause, Tate opened her envelope. She pulled out two sheets of beige stationary with red flowers trailing down the left side. She perused the first few lines, fought the instant rise of emotion, and blinked rapidly to clear the burn. "It's a letter."

Her voice was as faint as the sweet scent of oil. "Mom wrote us a letter."

"Sit down. Read it to us." Sami took her seat again at the table and placed the locket in front of her with care. Fiona sat beside her, still holding the grimoire.

Brit and Tate followed suit, and after a bracing breath, she began to read.

My dear daughters, as I write this to you, I am both fearful and sad. It breaks my heart that the last words you'll have from me are prompted by such terrible circumstances. You are too young to know what is happening, though I doubt you will ever truly understand or accept what I must do.

Tate stopped and took a drink of coffee. Was this a suicide note? If so, could she bear to read it?

Yes. She could. She had to.

If you've found this letter and the strongbox, then you have been visited by Rhiann, the same messenger who came to me.

This morning, as I stood on the cliffs to watch the dawn, Rhiann walked right out of the sunrise, every part of her as gold and pure as the day's new light. She gave me a missive from the goddess, the Dea Matrona.

She gave me a warning.

Hellana has come for you girls. She is a monster. How else could she see my sweet children as enemies who should be destroyed? Fiona is only a baby, but that won't stop Hellana. She is from another existence and has no compassion for our kind. So it is up to me to protect you, my daughters, no matter the cost.

Your grandfather and uncle Brit will tell you more. They will teach you all of the things I should have been able to teach you myself. I can only pray they will be able to keep you safe until the danger has passed, until you are old enough and fully prepared to defend yourselves.

"But we aren't," Fiona broke in, one hand resting atop the book while the fingers of the other drummed on the table. "We can't do anything." There was no blame or censure in her voice, only regret, and distress.

Sami put her hand over Fiona's to stop the tapping, but she spoke to Granddad and Brit. "That's twice tonight we've heard the name Hellana. Who is she? Why does she want to hurt us?"

Granddad shook his head. "I don't know."

When Tate and her sisters continued to stare at him, his face fell. "I swear. I don't know."

She hated that this obstruction had come between them, that the trust they had in their grandfather had been impeded for any reason.

Granddad gestured to the large book with his hands. "May I?" he asked Fiona.

"Of course." Blushing, as if ashamed to be having the same thoughts as Tate, Fiona passed him the grimoire.

After a minute of searching, their grandfather stopped on a page. "Here she is. Hellana. Your grandmother wrote of her. The date . . . yes, she included this information when your mother was only a year old."

He passed the open book back to Fiona. "She wrote this after learning of my mistake, my bargain with Emuirdane."

Tate stood and angled toward Fiona. There was a sketch of a woman whose hair—described as deep blue—flowed down to her hips. She was dressed in clothing reminiscent of a belly dancer, and her eyes, lined with kohl, had a flirtatious upturn at the corners. "Well," Tate said, "she doesn't look like a witch."

"Don't confuse the secret people with witches," Brit instructed. "As we said before, different groups, different terminology. But this Hellana, if she's from the farworld, like Emuirdane, she isn't human."

Sami poked Fiona's elbow. "Read."

"Oh. Okay." Fiona crinkled her brow. "It's long, so I'll summarize. Known as Hellana, *femeia dorit*. What?"

"The desirable woman," Brit supplied. His left brow winged up as he studied the rendering of her, the large lips and eyes, curvaceous body. "But why would she have come here looking for you three?"

"Let's see." Fiona cleared her throat. "From a wealthy Iele family, much desired, which we already know. Ah."

"What, Fee?" Sami was the one tapping the table now.

"Regardless of what this says, I refuse to feel sorry for her. She's the reason our mother is dead." Fiona pressed her lips until they whitened. "But apparently, she was taken as Emuirdane's bride. Grandmother underscored the word "taken" three times. In the side note here, she questions if this literally meant Hellana was forced to marry him."

Tate agreed with Fiona and couldn't drum up much sympathy. "What else does it say?"

"Not much. No mention of powers or vengeance. If Grandmother or Mom ever learned what Hellana wanted, they didn't include it here."

"We may have this all wrong." Sami cracked her knuckles and added a pop of her neck as she worked something out in her mind.

"How do you mean?" Granddad asked.

"If Hellana came here and Mom meant to face her, to stop her somehow . . ." Sami looked to Tate. "Maybe Mom didn't kill herself. Maybe she was murdered."

"No. I'm sorry, Sami." Granddad ran his hands over his face. "I followed her to the cliffs that night. I saw her jump."

"Nadia would have done anything to keep Hellana from harming your girls, even sacrificing herself to strengthen a protection spell." Brit pushed away from the table and paced to the counter where he leaned and stared out the window over the sink. "Whatever she did seems to be wearing off, because Hellana's come back. After the bloodhound attack, it's clear she wants you all dead."

"But why?"

"She may have been forced to marry Emuirdane," Granddad said. "If she hurts any of you, she hurts him. He's made it clear you're the only ones who can help him." There was no argument in their grandfather's tone, only defeat. "I should have never spoken to him. By saving your mother's life, I've condemned the three of you to his service."

"What could he possibly want from us?" Fiona asked.

"I can't imagine what his greatest desire might be. He has so much already." Granddad grew solemn. "Why can't they just leave you alone? You've done nothing to deserve this."

Tate touched his forearm. "But we're in this now, and even if Emuirdane and Hellana weren't interested in us, they've caused you and Brit so much pain. They've stolen from all of us."

"Right. And if I can't do magick, then just give me a sword like yours, Granddad." Sami leaned back in her seat, her legs bouncing with angry energy. "Hell, what am I saying? I'll *make* one."

"We still have to hear the rest of Mom's letter," Fiona said. "Go ahead, Tate."

Tate drew a deep breath, amazed by how this all centered on their mother. Normally, she did her best to forget, to avoid anything that would stir up memories.

But now she wanted to drink up everything she could. She wanted to know why their mother had been taken from them. Suicide or not, her actions had been coerced.

Tate read again.

I don't fully understand these instructions, but Rhiann insisted I leave these specific words behind for my daughters. I wish she and the goddess would fight Hellana and Emuirdane for us, but they seem to only watch and provide occasional guidance.

Rhiann told me to hide these items so that only the three of you together could find them.

I put every bit of my strength, love, and magick into this spell. I can only hope it works. I know in my heart this will be one of my final acts in this life, but it will be worth it if I can save my precious children.

The words she told me are on the next sheet. They are verbatim, exactly as she spoke them and instructed me to relay to you. Everything you need for what lies ahead is in this box. Except for your devotion to each other. Only you can bring your full power to this fight. You each have part of me in your blood. Times three, you are even stronger.

Use your sisterhood. It is your greatest weapon.

So be good girls, be sweet to each other, and live happy lives. The greatest magic comes from the peace within. Joy reveals the pathway to the source.

I have no regrets other than the loss of seeing you grow into women. I will miss so much, and I love you all more than can be expressed in this letter. Please tell my father and Brit what they've meant to me.

If I can find a way to look after you from beyond, I promise I will.

So when the wind brushes your hair and the sun kisses your cheeks, smile, my daughters, and know that is me.

Forever with love. ~~ Mom

With gentle fingers, Tate held the paper. More valuable than any treasure of gold or jewels.

She would have put money on herself to be emotional—as the oldest and the one with the most memories of their mother. Or Fiona, as she was the most tender.

But it was Sami who drew a shuddering breath and promptly broke into tears. She rested her head on her arms, face down to cover the flood.

"Oh, Sami." Fiona jumped up to embrace her sister. To comfort, as was her way.

With her own eyes watering, Tate set down the letter and wrapped her arms around them both. She was supposed to lead the way, to set the example. But for now, as they grieved, she would just be a sister.

Both their mother's spell and her words had stressed the importance of their being together.

And like a lamp clicking on in the dark, Tate knew. She wouldn't be leaving again.

Brit coughed and mumbled something about tissues, likely using the excuse so he could step out and hide his own raw pain.

Granddad didn't bother, but continued to sit, staring at his coffee. Tate slid her hand across the table and captured his.

Finally, Fiona pulled free, just in time to accept a tissue from Brit. "Thanks." She sniffed and lifted her chin to indicate the letter. "Let's finish it, Tate."

"Yes." With her eyes swollen and itchy, she picked up the papers, perused the second sheet. "There isn't much. Three lines written in a short stanza."

Gather the moons, the sisters three
To liberate the source
Set it free

Sami sat up straight and wiped her cheeks. "That's it?"

"Short and to the point," Tate said. "And cryptic."

"Maybe not." Fiona gestured to the locket in front of Sami. "She said everything we needed was in here. Can you open that up?"

"Sure." Sami used her thumb to flip the small latch and poured three perfectly rounded and shining pearls into her palm.

"Call me crazy," Fiona said, "but those look like—"

"Moons." Tate was surprised to feel laughter flow. "Good work, Fee."

"All right." Sami gingerly lifted a pearl to give each of her sisters. "We are clearly the sisters three, and the moons are now gathered." She stared down at her open palm and jiggled her hand as if to jumpstart the pearl.

Nothing happened, but then, Tate had no idea what to expect. People kept telling her she and her sisters had such great power.

But all she felt was a cool little ball in her hand.

"Maybe we should stand up and get closer to each other." Fiona moved to the floor space in front of the hearth. Tate and Sami followed.

They each held out a hand. With fingertips touching in the

middle of their small circle, pearls in open palms created a lovely tableau.

Tate searched for joy to open the path. Seconds passed. A minute. Still, nothing happened.

"We're supposed to have everything we need." Sami was the first to curl her fingers in and leave the circle. Her dark brown eyes fell to the final item extracted from the chest.

"We should check the box." Sami hovered over the wooden container.

"Those aren't for magick," Granddad said, but Sami was already lifting the lid.

"Wow." Three daggers rested on green velvet. Sami whistled her admiration and ran a reverent finger down one blade. "How did Mom do that?"

She picked up one of the daggers to examine their mother's work. "Veins of gold, and they've been seamlessly fused with the steel. High carbon." Sami nodded in approval. "Superior edge-holding and abrasion resistance."

With the crackling fire at her back, Tate drew a halting breath. Their mother had made them weapons?

Hand-to-hand combat weapons meant to draw blood. Meant to kill.

"Not for magick is right," Fiona said, biting her bottom lip and looking as concerned as Tate felt.

"The blades must contain iron," Granddad said.

"Of course. It's steel." Sami glanced to Granddad. "Is iron important?"

Brit held out his hand, and Sami passed the dagger to him. "Iron is known to poison the people of the farworld—the Fae, as they're known in other countries and cultures. Those who originate in the lands near Romania are also sensitive to gold."

Tate took one for herself, drawn to the marbleized metal, a gorgeous quality she'd never seen before. How *had* her mother done it? "I can't believe she made weapons for us when we were still only children."

Granddad sat back in his chair, his posture weary. "She knew you would one day face Emuirdane. We weren't sure what he wanted or if he would pose a threat, but she wanted you to be ready."

"These are gorgeous." Sami returned the dagger to the box with the others and closed the lid. "But I don't think they're going to help us with this poem or the pearls, the moons, whatever."

"We haven't even read the grimoire yet." Fiona placed her hands flat on the table on both sides of the large book.

"I'm going to need more coffee." Sami looked wistfully to the pot.

"Let's get started." Fiona opened the grimoire and flipped through the pages until she found something she liked. "Here. A spell to strengthen psychic ability. We certainly need answers, and it's a place to start."

Spinning on her heel, she rushed to the pantry and flung open the door. "I think we have a few of the ingredients. I'll start organizing whatever we have on hand."

Granddad rose from his chair, a bit more wobbly than normal. "Tomorrow, Fee. It's late, and you should get some sleep. The practice required of you and your sisters will be exhausting, in more ways than you can imagine."

He studied the open page and the spell she'd chosen. "We don't have the essentials you need, nor the tools, and you can't buy them tonight."

"Where do we get this stuff anyway?" Sami asked.

Brit put his empty mug in the sink. "We know of a place."

"We can still—" Fiona began.

"Please." Grandfather shook his head. "I am tired."

Tate went to him and took his arm to escort him. The man who'd valiantly fought demonic hounds now seemed thirty years older. "We do need to rest," she told him. "It's been a hard night."

"But we only have three days," Fiona said, her expression crestfallen.

Tate and Granddad kept walking, but she heard Sami's reply.

"Actually, less than that. It's two in the morning, Fee." Sami exhaled. "The countdown's already begun."

7

The next morning saw each of them up bright and early. Dew still lingered on the grass outside when Brit used the old brass key in his hand to unlock the attic door.

As far as Tate knew, the room had been locked for years, but she had vague memories of the open, airy space from her childhood. Dark wood tables and shelves, filled with books and strange implements she'd never been allowed to touch.

But she'd loved spending time here, curled up in a comfy chair to read while her grandmother sat at her desk beneath the high, rounded window. Most days, her grandmother had worked in an aged tome, bent over its timeworn pages.

Now Tate realized the importance of the older woman's research, the information she'd compiled, adding to the family history of the previous generations.

The forest-green book had been handed down the line to the Whiteburn sisters, and like their mother and grandmother before them, Tate, Sami, and Fiona would call upon this same collection of magickal data.

No one had been able to save their mother, but Tate was determined to write a different ending for her sisters.

She pictured cold, bracing winds chased inland by the punishing sea. She imagined her mother's hair whipping into her face. Had she thought of her daughters or called their names when she'd leapt to the unforgiving rocks below?

Oh, Mom. Tate's chest gave a long, hard squeeze. *What did you do for us?*

Unaware of how the room had affected Tate, Fiona brushed past her and skirted around Brit to take in the attic. The space spanned the length of the house with windows situated high above at each end.

Holding the grimoire to her chest, Fiona stopped in the very center and spun like a child in the garden. "This has been here the whole time?"

"I knew you'd love it," Brit said wistfully. "That's why we had to get creative. Keeping three inquisitive girls out of here proved to be a challenge."

Sami flattened her lips and put her hands on her hips as she surveyed the room. "So that's why you made sure we knew about the terrible spider infestation up here." She cocked a brow. "Was that even true?"

"I'm sure there were a few spiders." The corners of their uncle's mouth lifted suspiciously. "But to be sure, we kept the door locked and the lights empty of bulbs." He tugged one of Sami's long curls. "We knew the threat of darkness would keep you out if the bugs didn't."

"And you really thought keeping us ignorant of magick would keep us safe?" Fiona put her hands on her hips, a wrinkle of bafflement forming on her forehead.

"Or off Emuirdane's radar, at least."

"It was all I knew to do, Fiona." Granddad came through the door, stopping to run a finger through the dust on a decorative glass lampshade.

Dragonflies with purple wings. Tate recalled how fond her grandmother had been of the creatures and how the colors would brighten when the lamp was turned on.

"But he came anyway," Sami said. "Maybe we can find the key, and help him get back whatever was stolen from him."

Tate tried to believe it would be that simple, but even without psychic powers, she doubted Emuirdane would be so easily placated.

She rubbed her hands together. Sighed. "Where should we start?" With the sun in the sky, Tate was ready to make some progress.

Fiona carried the grimoire over to the desk but didn't lay down the book. "Um. We should clean first."

Guardian of her gift, she'd kept the book with her in her room last night, afraid to let it out of her sight. Just as Tate had put their mother's letter in a safe place and Sami had hidden the locket and pearls.

"Brit and I will take care of the cleaning," Granddad groused, never much one for housekeeping. "You girls have a more important task."

The shopping, Tate remembered. Though the items he and Brit had mentioned had never been on any of her grocery lists before.

"Ooh!" Fiona was pleased to skip the chore. "But before we go, I have a confession." She squeezed up her shoulders and sent her sisters a sheepish grin. "I looked through the grimoire last night. I couldn't help myself."

"What did you find?" Sami went to her as Fiona opened the book and balanced it on her arms.

"Well," Fiona said, "it's divided into sections, each with blank pages at the end for future entries." She pointed to the top where the heading read *Notes*. "The notes section reads like a journal of observations or important discoveries. Then there's a segment on the lore—where we read about Hellana—and one with spells and incantations, a mixture of both Romani and Celtic."

"Your grandmother's marriage to me was one reason we decided to come to America. Though we met in Wales, much of her family lived there as well. They did not approve of our union. They warned us not to mix the bloodlines."

Granddad's blue eyes went distant. "Maybe we should have listened."

Tate tsked. She'd had enough of this. "Would you make us disappear if you could? Erase our existence to keep us safe?"

Granddad pulled his head back in affront. "Of course not."

"Then can we please consider the subject closed? We don't blame you, and it hurts to see you blame yourself."

"I agree, "Brit said. "We did what we thought best, Dad. There's no going back."

"Only forward," Fiona added with a smile.

Sami frowned down at the book. "But we still have nothing to go forward with. As much as I hate to say it, Emuirdane was right. We need to practice."

"If we're a combination of bloodlines, then what are we?" Fiona asked

It was Brit who answered. "Witch, magi, priestess, mage. Take your pick." He pointed to a framed picture of a white-haired woman catching light in one hand while holding a bird on the tip of a finger with the other. "Many different phenomena are referred to as magick. It exists all around the world, and different cultures develop their own practices, create their own names."

Their uncle lifted the glass on a display case and retrieved a garnet-hued crystal. "Our family is blessed to have gifts from diverse societies. So while others see only a pretty rock," he offered the crystal to Tate, "we experience things on other levels."

She accepted the deep-red stone and shook her head at him. But then she sensed vibration in her palm. "I . . . but how? Last night, nothing happened with the pearls. I've touched crystals before and never felt anything like this."

"It's a drawing crystal, meant for training. It pulls on a practitioner's power, so they can feel it, know it's real."

"But before you can get started, there are things you'll need." Granddad stepped forward and handed Tate a piece of paper.

"Each of you should purchase one of the items marked with asterisks." He held up a finger. "It's important you choose them yourselves. Follow your instincts and see what calls to you."

"How will we know?" Sami asked.

"You won't know." Brit turned to her. "That's the first notion you should get out of your head." He tapped Sami's temple. "You won't know it. You'll *feel* it."

Tate must have looked doubtful, because her uncle came to her, closed her fingers around the red crystal so she could feel the hum, and told her, "Trust me."

~~~

They took the car to Agamont Park and then opted for a walk through the picturesque city of Bar Harbor. As girls, the three of them had enjoyed their jaunts to town, thrilling in the rush of tourist season, or delighting in the quieter months when locals ruled the streets.

Trees preened side by side in their rich autumn frocks, scarlet leaves blending into apple yellow. The vibrant hues provided the backdrop for rows of postcard-perfect shops.

Harsh winds blew in from the bottle-blue bay, so when they came to a coffee shop, Sami slowed and veered toward the glass doors. "The storm last night really brought in the cold. Let's stop to warm up."

"No. We can't waste any time." Fiona sidestepped her sister and kept going, head tucked into her coat collar to stave of the chilling breeze.

Sami's eyes bugged at the quick denial, and Tate almost laughed. "Wait, Fee." Now she did chuckle. "Wait."

Sami's routine was per her norm—no cares, no worries. Why do this minute what can be put off until next week? But Fiona was showing a previously tempered side of herself.

When it came to their newfound magick, she didn't defer to everyone else's wishes. She didn't waiver or try to appease. In fact, she was pretty straightforward. Downright obstinate.

And Tate couldn't be more thrilled.

"I think Fee's right." She followed after her youngest sibling, tossing over her shoulder to Sami, "We can stop for coffee on the way back."

Sami groaned and flopped her hands to her sides. "Fine, fine." She rushed to catch up to Tate, but rubbed her pink nose to prove how cold she was.

Tate latched onto Fiona, looping their arms together. Sami sidled up too, taking Fiona's other arm. Fiona swiveled her head between them and grinned, as if delighted her opinion, her wishes—which she rarely championed—had actually won out.

With her head ducked protectively, Tate kept an eye on the sidewalk as they hurried. Spying the painted curb of an intersection, she lifted her face to judge how far they had to go.

And stopped abruptly, skidding on the slick pavement.

"Hey!" Fiona protested the abrupt jerk, since her arm was still linked to Tate's. "What's the matter with you?"

Sami glanced at Tate looking across the street. "Oh," she dragged the word out. "I see the problem."

"Let's go inside." Tate tugged Fiona toward a candy store.

"But we agreed not to stop." Fiona pulled free. "Tate, what has gotten into you?" She followed Sami's line of sight, and her mouth formed a small moue. "Oh."

"Well, look there. It's Jack Helmsford." Sami's grin was pure mischief. "Let's wave him over."

"Sami . . . " Tate growled, easing behind Fiona but keeping a watchful eye on the man as he made his way around the opposite corner. *Please let him turn. Don't let him walk this way.*

She couldn't help noticing that Jack still wore his favored jeans and flannel shirt, a delicious combo of working-man-meets-male-model. His blonde hair just a bit too long, he tossed the bangs out of his eyes in an old habit. The familiar move was a quick punch to her gut.

"I still talk to him now and then," Sami said. She had always been Jack's biggest cheerleader. Maybe she still was.

Tate and Jack had loved young and loved blindly, as innocents often do. But years had passed, and when Tate had moved away, she'd felt it best to end the relationship. Cut all ties that might reel her back to a place she couldn't live.

Yet another decision she and her sister didn't see eye-to-eye on.

"We're talking about doing an exhibition together." Sami droned on as if all the blood hadn't drained from Tate's head. Like seeing Jack hadn't pulled the plug. "You know, something with a catchy title, a play on wood and metal."

Tate frowned as her sister's rambling finally registered. "An exhibition? He's still doing that?"

"Wipe that disdain from your tone." Sami bristled. "I'm honored that he would even consider sharing space with me at a showing. His work is highly sought-after, and it sells."

"For a lot of money," Fiona added, her wide eyes focused on Tate as she nodded.

"Seriously?" Tate remembered the wooden bowls and small trinkets Jack used to make, but she'd never tell Sami she still had the ring he'd given her. The smooth, simple band had been the stuff of youthful and romantic dreams.

Before reality and adulthood got in the way.

"Yep. He's a natural talent," Sami said. "Good with his hands."

Tate knew that to be *very* true. She had a vision of Jack, smiling down on her, golden hair mussed. The imagery made a place in her chest flutter.

"You could say his work elevated, took on deeper, more meaningful undertones," Sami motioned to Tate with her chin, "after you left."

"What's that supposed to mean?"

"Aw, well." Sami blew into her balled-up hands, ignoring the question, and Tate's irritation. "It wouldn't have worked out between you two anyway."

Tate opened her mouth, inhaled.

But Fiona grabbed her hand and then Sami's. "Guys, not now. We need to keep good energy flowing between us for what we're about to do. Jack Helmsford is as much a fixture in this town as the lampposts. He isn't going anywhere.

"We, however," Fiona lowered her voice with meaning, "only have three days."

"Good point." Sami nodded.

Jack had made that turn after all, so Tate was safe to proceed. As they resumed their trek, she sniffed and cut her eyes to Sami. In the spirit of good energy, there was one thing she had to say. "You know very well that I respect your work, Sami. I don't disdain artists."

"No. Just Jack."

"That's not true either. I guess . . . I just don't think of him that way."

"Come on, Tate. I've told you."

"I know. You're right." Tate had listened, but for self-preservation, she'd tuned out anything having to do with the boy—the man— who'd shared half the pain of her broken heart.

The truth was, she didn't know him now or what he was truly capable of. Jack had grown up, just as she had, and their worlds didn't revolve around each other anymore.

They hadn't in a long time.

Tate fell silent, wishing the autumn wind would carry away her bittersweet memories of the past. In addition to feeling the mist in the air, she shivered inside as well.

Soon Fiona paused to look up at a wooden sign swinging in the breeze. "This is the place."

"It's a candle store." Sami peered through the large window. "I don't think I've been here before."

"Me either." Fiona furrowed her brows. "And I love candles."

"Granddad and Brit probably did something to keep us away from here too." Tate reached for the curved brass handle. "Maybe they cast an anti-magick spell on us."

But if they had, that enchantment was surely gone, because as soon as she crossed the threshold, she felt it. *Magick.*

Along with the sweet smell of scented wax, another sensation surrounded her. She couldn't put words to the feeling. It was as if a sixth sense she'd never known before was suddenly alert and searching.

"Do you feel that?" Fiona closed her eyes and let her head fall back. "Mmm . . . better than a hot bubble bath."

"Oh, I feel it." Sami squirmed. "But I'm not sure I'm comfortable with whatever just rolled through me."

Tate was somewhere in the middle of her sisters' reactions, intrigued but cautious.

A woman with fair hair was pulling jars of bright green wax from a box to stock the shelves. Her arm froze mid-lift when she noticed them, and her eyes smiled just before her lips.

"Well, well, well. Look who finally came out of the broom closet." She returned the candle to the box and walked toward them, clasping her hands. Her light laughter was somehow comforting.

Sami edged up to Tate's side, but Fiona met the woman halfway and extended her hands. The two greeted each other like long-lost friends. "We never knew we were in one," Fiona said.

"I guess we're in the right place," Sami mumbled.

Tate glanced around but saw only candles. "Apparently. Though this isn't what I pictured."

Fiona lifted her nose and sniffed. "What smells so good?"

"Oh, that's Honeycrisp Apple," the woman said. "One of my

fall favorites." With a shrewd tilt of her head, she stepped to Tate to shake her hand. All business now, where with Fiona, she'd been giddy as a schoolgirl.

"Tate," she said, beaming. "I'm Kat, and it's a real pleasure to meet you."

Lastly, she spoke to Sami. "I have one of your pieces, you know. You have a real gift for balancing heavy and light aspects. The contrast is striking yet subtle . . ." Kat smiled and shook her head. "I just don't know how you do it."

"Oh. You do? Um, thanks," Sami babbled, taken off-guard by the praise.

"Of course, your Uncle Brit had to buy the artwork for me." Kat's friendly face fell into disgruntled lines. "Since I've been banned from contacting the three of you for fear it might jar your magick into action."

She waved a dramatic hand. "As if I don't have any more control than that. Now, I know why you're here, so come on back." She spun around in her cherry red flats and waved them to follow as she walked to the rear of the store.

She led them through a door and into a stockroom, shelves all around with more boxes like the one she'd been unpacking. Next they traversed a short hallway with an office on one side and a very feminine bathroom opposite.

The scent of Honeycrisp was here as well.

They came to another door, this one indigo with a metallic sun and moon decoration. Kat wiggled her light brows and pushed it open.

The space was the same size as the candle showroom, but the mood was markedly altered. Rich colors set off darker shelves, as opposed to the honey-toned wood and glass out front.

"Everything here is also merchandise." Kat flicked a switch, and lamps cast soothing triangles of gold into each corner. "I don't advertise, though. Some customers wouldn't understand."

The candles displayed here weren't in holders or jars, but loose in cardboard containers, still separated by color but with a handmade quality. Jewel-toned velvet draped various tables that were scattered with stones and crystals, similar to those in the attic at home.

Candles and crystals. Tate put her fingers to the base of her throat. How her world had changed in less than a day.

But at least they could mark two things off of the list Granddad had given them.

"Here are the knives." Sami—drawn to metal—had a finger placed on the glass of a display case.

"Athames, dear," Kat corrected. "Or arthames, if you prefer the ancient name."

Tate breathed in through her nose, trying to realign her new reality. They already had daggers. Tilting her head, she wondered if their mother had warmed Fiona's baby bottle before heading out back to fashion her a weapon against Romanian fairies.

"Before we go any further, you should select one of earth's minerals." Kat's voice dragged Tate back to the discussion. "Stone or crystal, it doesn't matter."

Their new acquaintance stood beside a red-cloaked table and waited for them to join her. "Once I see where your energies guide you, I can make proper suggestions for your other tools."

Fiona threaded her fingers together and rose up on her toes. Tate hadn't seen her this spirited since their trip to that specialty culinary store in Portland.

"I know this is exciting, but please take your time." Kat put a hand on Fiona's shoulder.

Sami stuck her hands in her pockets as she moved to a table of stones. "What do we do?"

Kat pressed a finger to her lips. "The less instruction I provide, the better."

"Remember what Uncle Brit said." Fiona was drawn to a table

with crystals glittering atop royal blue. "You will feel it."

"Brit—" Kat began, her fine features tightening. "I mean, your uncle is correct." She firmed her mouth and fluttered her eyes as if doing her best to withhold further comment.

Tate's brows winged up, but she said nothing. Besides, she was supposed to be "feeling" a rock.

Fiona zeroed straight in, picking up a crystal with stripes of dark blue, purple, and deep yellow. "This is mine."

"Ah. Blue John Fluorite." Kat smiled. "From *bleu-jaune*, meaning blue yellow, as the French miners named it. The most sought-after fluorite in the world, and very soothing for sensitives." She angled her head to Fiona. "Which I believe you are."

"She's sensitive all right," Sami joked, holding her hands up when Fiona shot her an evil eye.

"That crystal is said to be a catalyst for growth, is a strong teaching stone, and may improve the owner's ability to heal." With her piece said, Kat looked to Sami, who lifted a shoulder. So the storeowner settled on Tate.

"No pressure," Kat said, patting the air. "Take your time."

No pressure, Tate thought. When she had no idea which table she should even check first.

Recalling the energy she'd felt in the red stone that morning, she began a slow tour around the edge of the room, hoping a similar buzz would reach out to her, that something would "call to her."

After one full circuit, she was ready to make Sami try.

Then something caught her eye. And she knew without a doubt that she would choose based on visual interaction instead of kinesthetic. She would see instead of touch.

Through shelves in the middle of the room, she noticed a soft lavender glow. Just like the wings of her grandmother's glass dragonflies.

Her heart thudded as if she were on a first date, and the trust, the affection she felt for that purple light was undeniable. The minerals lay atop a white velvet spread, and Tate grasped her chosen crystal with complete confidence.

She turned to Kat like a pupil awaiting a grade.

"Tanzanite. Good choice." Kat casually crossed her arms. "A stone of magick to help with spiritual awareness and psychic insight. It turns your mind to pleasant things. Helps you slow down. For this reason, it's often called the workaholic's stone."

Sami burst out laughing at the last. "Tate, you definitely made the right choice." She rocked back on her heels, thoroughly enjoying the fact that the arcane energies had pegged Tate so accurately.

"Your turn, Sami." Tate held her Tanzanite between her thumb and finger, showing off her prize and the task her sister had yet to complete.

"Fine." Sami shook out her hands, bounced on the balls of her feet.

"You aren't going into a boxing ring," Tate said.

Sami shrugged. "You sure about that?"

Tate thought of Emuirdane and the mysterious Hellana. Sami had a point.

Taking deep breaths, Sami held out her hand like a metal detector, floating her open palm over the tables. Tate wasn't sure, but she thought she heard her humming.

The strange practice must have worked, since Sami stopped beside the fourth collection she inspected. Tate craned her neck. Those didn't look like crystals.

Sami circled her hand a few more times over a particular pile of stones. Black stones, round, smooth, and shiny with barely visible veins in a creamy color. She dove in and picked.

Kat tilted her head, but then she quickly pasted a smile on her face. "Schorl. Also known as black tourmaline." She didn't elaborate.

"What does mine do?" Sami was eager now.

"That particular stone can help cleanse your aura. It's a purifying mineral capable of deflecting or transforming negative energy." Kat ended on a positive note. "It can also help you obtain higher levels of awareness."

Sami seemed nonplussed. "A protective stone that also makes me more aware. Cool."

"Yay." Fiona lifted her fists and shook them with unrestrained enthusiasm. "Now we're getting somewhere. And doesn't it feel good?" She gazed at her crystal and stroked it lovingly.

Though not experiencing quite the same passion, Tate had to agree. Having the crystal in her hand was a comfort. She even felt more powerful.

And they hadn't even gotten to wands, candles, or any of the other list items yet.

She glanced at her sisters, proud to share this moment with them. "It does feel good, Fee. It really does."

Sami released a soft breath. "Yeah. But more than that," she looked to Tate, "it feels *right*."

8

After an hour of browsing, marveling, and learning a few tips from Kat, Tate and her sisters had full bags of magickal toys. Tate also chose a couple of pumpkin spice candles from the front showroom.

Standing at the counter and waiting for Fee to finish checking out, Tate had to admit that the female camaraderie and enticing scent of apples and herbs had done wonders for their moods. Even Sami was looking forward to working her first spell.

She and Tate were finally getting a taste of the exhilaration Fiona had been riding since last night. And in a complete role-reversal, they were letting their little sister guide them.

Kat had been so happy to finally get to know the "Whiteburn girls," she'd insisted on making gifts of their stone and crystals.

Fiona gave their newfound friend and mentor a hug. "Thank you so much."

"Yeah, thanks," Sami said. "Too bad you can't grab a coffee with us."

"Some other time." Kate gave Sami a smile and patted Tate's arm.

"I'd like that," Tate said, and meant it. "You've made all of this much easier, Kat."

"That's what I'm here for." She glanced outside and narrowed her gaze at the sky. "Don't tell me it's going to rain again."

"Probably Hellana acting up," Sami joked.

The creamy skin of Kat's faced turned ashen. "What did you say?"

Tate gripped the handle of her bag. "You didn't know?" The apprehension in Kat's expression crushed her previous cheer. With all the learning and shopping, they hadn't discussed their little family problem with her.

"Granddad and Brit sent us here because we have to prepare," Fiona said. "It's the only reason they told us . . . what we are."

"They didn't have a choice," Sami added. "Not after the bloodhounds and Emuirdane showed up."

Kat's fingers fluttered at her throat. "Emuirdane came here? From the farworlds?"

"Don't you mean farworld? Singular?" Tate zeroed in on her wording.

"It's complicated," Kat said, hedging. She swayed forward a bit. "But you actually saw him? And Hellana?"

"Only Emuirdane." Tate started to set her bags down to help Kat. "You should sit."

"I'm fine. Really." When she swung her eyes to Tate, her gaze sharpened, her shoulders drew back.

And suddenly the sweet shopkeeper appeared rigid, formidable. "Listen to me. Be very careful with them, Emuirdane especially. Never accept a favor from him, no matter how small. Don't allow him to give you anything."

She gripped Tate's fingers. Hard. "*Anything*. No food or drink. Not a single bite."

"We won't," Tate assured her, silently promising herself that more conversations with Kat were in order. She clearly didn't feel the need to protect them from the truth.

"Our grandfather made a deal with him years ago," Fiona said, her lips pressed tight. "We already owe him our help to pay the debt."

"Oh." Kat exhaled and closed her eyes. "This explains so much."

Tate studied the quickly-darkening atmosphere outside. The hairs of her nape stood at attention and tingled. "We should we hurry."To Kat she said, "Is there anything more we need to know?"

"Plenty."

Tate had to admire the woman's frankness.

"But another time. For now, remember what I told you about taking gifts. I don't care if he tries to toss you a pretty pebble. Don't catch it."

"He healed us," Fiona said. "Me and Tate."

"Did he offer, and you accept?"

Tate shook her head side to side. "We didn't know what he was going to do or that he even could. We were stunned, injured." Worry swirled in Tate's chest. Did she and Fiona owe even more now?

"Then you should be fine. The Iele are tricky, but they must play by certain rules."

Kat's head jerked when a woman across the street opened a cherry-red umbrella. She'd grown anxious, jumpy. And her dread was seeping into Tate.

"It's starting to rain," Kat said. "You should go before things get worse."

"Will you be safe?" Sami must have picked up on the same fear-tinged undercurrents.

"Yes. I'm just taken aback." Kat opened the door for them, but when she did, a harsh wind blasted inside, throwing the door wide and shoving the women backward. The store lights flickered, and every burning candle snuffed out.

Tate squinted against the wind sandblasting her face, her eyes.

"Shut the door," Fiona said, placing both hands on the frame to push.

"No. Wait." Kat grasped a pendant hanging from her neck. She lifted her other hand, palm forward, to catch the already-waning breeze. Her hair lifted at the tips, and orange light emanated from the fingers curled around the necklace. "The strength is dying now, but the force behind it is powerful. And angry."

"Hellana?" Sami asked.

"I'm not sure. But the wind," she looked upward, "those clouds. They carry hate, a bad omen." Kat gave Tate a little shove of encouragement. "You three need to get back home. Now."

~~~

Brit was looking out the kitchen window when they pulled into the drive and was out the door, headed their way, before Tate could switch off the ignition

He opened the back door of the car to help Sami with bags. "Are you all okay?" he asked as the wind screeched and flattened his black hair to his head. "I should have gone with you."

Sami stood, battling to keep her own hair out of her face. "Or maybe not." She was tall but still had to look up at her uncle. "If you'd been there, you might have kept Kat from telling us what we needed to know."

Fiona shook her head at her uncle and pursed her lips, raising her voice to carry. "If you and Granddad want to protect us, you need to tell us everything."

Brit scowled and eyed the ugly sky. The same brewing cauldron of clouds had followed them home from Kat's shop, churning and building upon itself. Now that they were out in the elements, the wind slashed and whipped. Then the rain started, tiny drops hitting like finger-thumps to the flesh.

Brit kicked the door shut. "Inside."

When a droplet struck her in the eye, Tate agreed. The safety and warmth of the house was a smart idea. Plus, they could interrogate the men of the family better without the tempest howling in their ears.

Once jackets were removed and hung in the mudroom, the

three women surrounded Brit like a small mob. Granddad hurried in from the parlor just in time, unaware he was about to be charged as a co-conspirator.

"What did Kat say that you think we kept from you?" Brit asked, drawing his father's frown.

Sami held both hands out, shaking with agitation. "That we shouldn't accept anything from Emuirdane. No favors or food." She scrunched her shoulders and her nose at the same time and held up her hands. "No food? What does that even mean?"

Granddad blew through his lips. "Oh, dear." Then he patted his hands at her in a tut-tut manner. "You're right, Sami. We should have told you, but we didn't purposely leave it out. With the short time we've been given, all the surprises . . ."

"What Kat said is true," Brit cut in. "And she was right to do so. I should have made certain things clear before you left the house today. I apologize."

"And I," his father said. "I'll give you the high points on the dangers of Iele, but then you really should get started upstairs." Granddad clasped his hands into a ball. "All right. First rule." He didn't bother to sit but started reeling off guidelines.

Well, Tate thought, they'd asked for it.

"Never knowingly accept a gift or favor from the Iele. They use such exchanges to control us mortals, either by demanding repayment in some way—or, in the case of food or drink—exerting control over a person's actions."

"How?" Sami asked, ready to dig for every kernel of information. "Poison?"

Granddad held up a finger. "Just the high points for now. Secondly," he continued, "remember that when dealing with an Iele, or any Fae for that matter, what you see is not always real. The magick people originated the skill known as glamour. The ability was first used to confuse and deceive, often for personal gain. The Iele are masters at this."

"I thought glamour was used to change your own appearance," Tate said, recalling movies and books she'd read.

"Some humans are capable of this," Brit explained, "but the Iele can do much more."

"Like what?"

"They can alter your perception of reality."

Tate gestured. "The storm outside?"

"No, that's real." Brit glanced out the bay window to the dark weather. "Hellana has quite the temper, it seems."

"Which brings us to the last. A point I've wondered over." Granddad rubbed his chin, his silver brows clamping down and in to create a V. "Iele cannot attack mortals without just cause. It is forbidden."

Tate froze, her mouth dropping open. "Then how do you explain last night? We were definitely attacked."

"That's what troubles me." Granddad met her gaze. "If I fail to repay Emuirdane, he will be justified in his retaliation. But Hellana . . . we owe her nothing."

"Then why? How can she?" Tate, rarely at a loss for words, spit out short, drilling questions. Were there laws for this other world, these *other* species? And if so, how could she use them to protect her family?

"I can't honestly say. But there will be consequences for her actions. She must have a very good reason for taking such risks."

"So who do we call in the farworld? Can't we report her to the authorities or something?" Sami, blasé despite the serious topic, went to the counter and lifted the lid of the glass cake dish. "Hey, Fee. Do you mind?"

"No, no. In fact, I could use a sugar boost." Fiona set her bag on the table and opened a cabinet for the plates. Over her shoulder, she continued to grill Granddad and Brit. "If we can't safely leave the house, how are we supposed to find the key?"

"There is some good news," Brit said, heading to the coffee

maker.

"You read my mind," Sami interrupted with a half-grin. She and Brit both suffered from an apparently-crippling java addiction.

"The good news?" Tate prodded.

"Yes, yes. I believe Hellana's power, her reach, if you will, is limited." He circled his hand as if searching for the right explanation. "She is nearby, but she's only projecting. I sense her magick is being held back or restrained, so she sends a storm to threaten us instead."

"She can't come here?" Fiona asked.

"No." Granddad hummed in his throat before clarifying, "We don't believe so, no."

Brit, scooping grounds into the filter, paused to say, "We performed a search spell and set protection around the property while you were gone. We weren't able to pinpoint Hellana's location, but she's close. Still, her presence isn't as powerful as it was last night.

"She used a lot of energy sending those hounds, the fog, and her voice," Brit continued. "But she failed, and is weaker now."

"She blew a fuse," Sami said, gesturing with the cake knife. "But Kat also said that burst of wind at the store was losing power as we stood there. So that tracks with the theory."

Fiona took two plates with purple slices and carried them to the table. "You don't think Hellana's a threat anymore?"

"I didn't say that." Brit's voice was stern. "You still need to be wary when you go out of the house. And especially when it's time to search for the key. If Hellana isn't throwing her magick at us, it's only because she's storing it up."

Tate stilled. "She's saving it for us. For when we're forced to venture out." She and her sisters, novices to be sure, would have to face a supernatural being who wanted to kill them. In less than two days.

Fiona and Sami both looked wan, as if thinking the same thing.

Fiona busied herself with another couple of plates. "This protection spell you created, how does it work?"

Brit lifted his hand, and Tate felt a silky, warm pulse of energy spread throughout the room. She sighed, as did Fiona, before the soothing current rolled outward, expanding beyond the walls, across the yard, and all the way into the forest of red pines.

How do I know that? Some part of her had traveled with the spell, sensing every particle of grass or pine needle it had touched.

"Wow." Sami dropped her arms.

"We may not be as powerful as Nadia was, or you are," Brit grinned, "but Dad and I do have our ways."

Tate hugged herself, feeling calmer, inexplicably comforted. "I don't know what exactly just passed through me, but it was nice."

"Because it's our family magick," Granddad said. "If Hellana steps onto our land, however, she'll have a very different reaction."

"And Emuirdane?" Sami asked.

Granddad's face fell. "No. We geared the enchantment to Hellana only. She is the greater danger right now, and we couldn't spare any magick to ban Emuirdane."

"We'll just hope he stays on our side then." Tate took a seat and thanked Sami when she brought over a mug of steaming black coffee, no cream or sugar. Just how she liked it.

"He did say he was our protector," Tate reminded them. "But he seems to want to follow up on our . . . quest, as he called it." She stared into the dark reflection in her cup, recalling Emuirdane's words from the previous night. His actions. "He has something more at stake."

"Finding Hellana?" Sami suggested. "She is his wife."

Granddad chuffed as if she'd said something funny. "A wife he's clearly having some trouble with, else he wouldn't allow her to threaten you girls."

"Whether Emuirdane truly means to watch over you or not, you'll eventually have to leave our land." Brit's expression was grim.

Tate met his eyes, nodded. "We'll be past the boundary of the protection spell."

"Yes. The weapons Nadia made won't be enough. You'll need more than iron and gold to defend yourselves against the likes of Hellana."

"We'll need magick. That's what you mean." When everyone was seated at the table, Tate scooped up a bite of cake. "So let's charge up with sugar and caffeine and see if we can get our new toys to work."

9

The attic was transformed.

Tate and her sisters made sounds of delight as they entered to find the dusty, cobweb-ridden storage room spotless, with curiosities on display fit for the pages of any children's fantasy book. Wood gleamed, brass shone, and glass shimmered, the scent of citrus mixing deliciously with oiled leather.

High above their grandmother's desk, the round window cast a unique sunshadow through its four panes, creating a pale yellow circle on the hardwoods with a cross in its center.

"There," Fiona pointed to the pattern. "That's where we should set up."

"On the floor?" Sami curled her lip.

Tate nudged her with an elbow. "It's clean now. No spiders."

Sami rolled her eyes.

"And," Fiona added, "we can form a circle, sit in relaxed poses."

"We aren't doing yoga, Fee."

"Actually," Granddad said, correcting Sami, "she's not far off. The three of you should be close together to start, and a circle is always best. Plus," now he twisted up his face as if he didn't want to say the rest, "you're likely to be at this for a while. And sitting is better."

"Because you're going to get tired," Brit said. "Sooner than you think."

"But we have stones now. And," Sami opened her bag as if

offering proof, "other shortcuts."

"Agh, Sami." Granddad put a hand to his chest. "You'll have a much harder time with an attitude like that."

"I thought that's what these were for." She lifted a shoulder and reached in to retrieve her Schorl. The black stone was wrapped in paper, a protection stone being protected.

"Yes, yes. They are instruments meant to help you, but magick, true magick, comes from within." Granddad lifted a finger. "Like a bicycle. The mechanics can take you places more quickly, but not unless you supply the energy.

"But first," he added, "you must practice finding your center, the core where you power resides. It may be different for each of you, but to do magick, you must be able to pull from that place. Every time, and with haste."

"In other words," Tate supplied, "if we get into trouble, we won't have time to sit on the floor and wait for it to happen."

"Exactly." Brit nodded. "The key is to relax. Let it flow from its point of origin. When you need it in the future, you'll know where to find it."

"Can we light candles to help us start?" Fiona asked, biting her bottom lip like a student afraid to fail an exam.

"Whatever works for you." Granddad crossed to a chair and sat. Leaning forward, he made a go-ahead gesture with his hand.

"Should we use our crystals?" Fiona asked.

"Let's not." Tate removed hers from her bag and set it on the table nearest them. "Just us first. See what we can do."

After her sisters placed their stones next to hers on the table, they all took up positions around the sun-lit circle on the floor. They glanced at each other, then to Brit and Granddad, before closing their eyes one by one.

Tate breathed deeply. She tried to let her inner magick flow.

But all she could think about were the two sets of eyes burning holes into her back. Eventually, she exhaled and looked back to the men.

"We're watching," her grandfather assured her.

Tate hated to hurt his feelings, but . . . "That's the problem."

"Yeah," Sami said. "Pressure much?"

Fiona sent him an apologetic smile but said, "Uh-huh."

"Fine, fine." Granddad tapped his cane and got up. "Come on, son. He waved his hand at Brit. "Let's leave them to it." He harrumphed, loudly, for their benefit. "I forgot how picky *fermecători* could be. They've got your grandmother's Romanian ways, that's for sure."

Tate stifled laughter but only tamped it down to a slow rumble. "What did he call us?"

"I have no idea." Sami rubbed her belly. "But it made me think of Italian food. Think we could talk Brit into cooking, since we'll be busy?"

"Right." Fiona could barely speak through her chuckles. "We'll be working hard, trying to become good cacciatore."

"Now I'm really getting hungry." Sami turned down her lips. "But later." She cleared her throat, rolled her shoulders. "I'm ready to get to work."

"I'll light that candle. Something to help us relax." Fiona went back to her bag and rummaged through it until she found the one she wanted. "I read in the grimoire that lavender has a calming effect." Fiona lit the wick of a wide pillar of gentle bluish-purple.

"Do you have the locket?" Tate asked Sami.

Her sister pulled the silver chain from beneath her shirt until the round filigree locket appeared. "Let's still try to find our power first. I don't want to rush it."

Tate studied the necklace. "I don't want to be disappointed again either, but time is running out."

"I know, I know." Sami held up her hands and waved them in a back-off motion. "Let's just focus on one thing at a time, okay? Trust me. I work with dangerous things every day. It's not smart to get ahead of yourself."

Tate considered the damage that heated metal could do to flesh, or the spinning blade of Sami's saws. In this, she would defer to her sister. "You're right. One thing at a time."

Sami's eyes widened. "Did you just tell me I'm right about something?"

"Oh, for pity's sake." Fiona bent her head and put her hands to her forehead. "Not now."

"Hey, I was only joking." Sami dusted her hands together. "Okay. I'm closing my eyes. I'm breathing."

With a grin whisping over her lips, Tate did the same, recalling Kat's instructions from before. She'd told them not to block the world around them, but to let it speak to them instead.

To listen for what they'd never heard before.

Picturing the air she breathed rolling back and forth through her body, in and out, Tate let her feet relax, then her legs, and all the way up to her shoulders and neck.

Granddad was right. This was similar to yoga.

She opened herself up to the sounds, smells, and textures all around her. Again, she followed the air with her mind, down, down, rippling with golden waves of light.

Soon the atmosphere and its stimuli grew in strength. They began to tug at her consciousness. The floor creaked as Sammy adjusted her position. The flame of the candle on the table crackled and hissed. And outside, clouds puffed and shifted form in response.

Tate crinkled her nose but kept her eyes closed. Clouds puffing in response? Ridiculous. Impossible.

As soon as the negative thoughts entered her head, her purple crystal called out from across the room. Destroying her state of relaxation, Tate jerked her face toward the Tanzanite.

"What is it?" Sammy asked, sensing the movement.

"I . . . My . . ." Was she really about to say this? She swallowed.

"Well, my crystal just . . . chastised me."

"Really?" Fiona followed her gaze to the three stones. "Mine has been whispering, but it only makes me feel warm inside. And safe."

"Maybe I shouldn't have gotten a rock," Sami groused, "because I haven't heard anything."

"Just give it time," Fiona said, setting her hand on Sami's knee. "We just got started."

"That's not true." Tate noted the hands on the brass clock sitting on a bookshelf. "We've been sitting here for almost an hour."

"No way." Fiona whipped around to confirm the time before looking down to the floor. The bright circle of midday sun had drifted farther across the wood.

Sammy unfolded herself and stood in one smooth move. "That clenches it. I'm going to hold my stone. See if it helps." She picked up the black Schorl with her fingers, but said, "Hey!" and dropped it back to the table.

She looked down and shook her fingers. "Shit."

"Are you all right?" Fiona leapt up and grabbed Sami's hand.

"I'm okay. It was hot. Not hot enough to burn, but it surprised me." She held out her palm for inspection and jumped when a white flame flickered to life in its center. "Wha—"

"Sami!" Fiona gaped. "Does it hurt? What does it feel like?"

"Um. Hard to describe."

"Well try." Fiona waited but Sami only lifted her shoulder.

Fiona opened her own palm, stared hard, squinted, but nothing happened.

After a moment, she dodged her eyes back and forth from where Sami stood, still admiring the fire, to where Tate sat cross-legged on the floor. Then she hooked Sami's elbow to pull her back to the circle. "Quick. Let's try the pearls while you're connected to the magick."

Sami rooted herself to the spot. When Fiona cast her a quizzical look, she reached back. "I still need the stone." Gingerly, she picked up the smooth, round Schorl with her fire-free hand, and after testing it by rolling it between her fingers, she nodded. "Still warm, but not too hot to hold."

She came over and plopped back down. Eyes filled with regret, she curled her fingers and doused the white flames. "I hope I can do that again."

Fiona, practically trembling with excitement, gestured to the locket and pearls within. "You will. But the pearls are priority."

"I agree, but we should try something different." Tate accepted her pearl when Sami handed it over, but set it on the floor in the center of their circle. She reached for her sisters. "Sami's in tune with her magick, so maybe she can stimulate ours too."

Fiona grasped Tate's extended hand. "Excellent idea."

Sami shrugged. "Guess it can't hurt."

So with hands joined to create an unbroken circuit, they closed their eyes again. And fell immediately into serenity. Tate's hope soared. They'd already mastered the drop into a trancelike state.

She pictured her sisters' hands melding into hers, the energy traveling from Sami to her to Fiona before arriving back at its origin. As soon as she conjured the imagery, she felt the warmth.

"It's working," Fiona whispered.

Tate almost shushed her, but her words didn't seem to interrupt the power flowing between them. The sensation of heat only amplified, the speed increasing as it raced through their joined bodies.

Tate felt a tingle at the base of her skull. She turned her inner eye toward it and light erupted, so bright she opened her eyes in response. "I found it. My center."

Fiona squeezed Tate's hand, a little too hard, so her knuckles scrunched together. "Mine's in my heart." Her green eyes blazed.

"My hands," Sami said. "That's why I called the flame so easily." She tossed her head back and laughed at the ceiling. "My hands."

A quick stab of heat had Tate jerking away, breaking the

connection. "Ow, Sami. What did you do?"

"It's just a little fire. And I didn't mean to."

"Well, get control of it before you hurt someone."

Sami narrowed her eyes, ground her teeth together.

"Where's your source, Tate?" Fiona was on her knees, staring down at her pearl.

"In my head."

"What a shocker. Tate's got a big head." Sami slapped a hand to her mouth. "Um. I don't know why I said that."

Tate began to speak, the tone forming on her tongue snide and cruel, but she took note of the darkened room and her eyes traveled to the brass clock again. "Oh. I know why. I know exactly why we're both so irritable."

Sami tracked her line of sight. "It's almost six? Are you kidding me? I swear, we only held hands for a minute." She stood, visibly shaken by the loss of time. "I need a break."

Fiona huffed and grabbed Sami's leg. "Wait. Just one more try."

"No, Fee. We've been at this for hours." Sami flung a hand to the window, "The sun is setting, and I'm starving."

"How can you think about your stomach right now?"

"I'm thinking about not passing out on the floor. Is that okay with you?" Sami ripped her leg free and, still muttering to herself, marched from the attic to clomp downstairs.

"What a grouch." Fiona glared at the door, even after Sami had vacated. "She's not taking this seriously enough." She glanced to Tate. "You should tell her."

"Me?" Tate gaped. "You're the one always telling us not to fight, and now you want me to wave a red flag in her face? My telling Sami what to do will piss her off more. If you want to get her to do something, tell her yourself."

Tate pushed up from the floor, turned her back on Fiona, but paused before stomping away. She had the urge to storm out like Sami had, but such hotheaded behavior was very unlike her.

She eased around to find Fiona staring up at her with a glower. And *that* was very unlike Fee.

"I'm sorry," Tate said. "I don't know what's wrong with me." In a gesture of cease-fire, she held out a hand to help her sister up.

"I'm sorry too." Fiona channeled her elfin grin, but it was limp. "We should all take five. Get some water and a snack. Maybe then we'll be more like our old selves."

"I hope so."

"Sami made fire," Fiona reminded her, optimism threaded through her sweet voice. "And we each found our centers. That's got to count for something."

"Yes. It does." Tate forced a smile to hide her worry. She couldn't help thinking about the pearls lying cool and silent on the wood floor. She didn't know what they were for, or what she and her sisters were supposed to do with them.

Day one of three was fading fast. If they didn't figure out the pearls by the third day, then . . . well, she couldn't imagine what might happen.

But a prelude consisting of flesh-tearing bloodhounds and Hellana's evil laughter didn't bode well.

Silently, she followed Fiona from the attic, telling herself she was just tired. Granddad had warned them, but she'd never anticipated how exhausting magick could be. Her knees were even creaky and sore from holding the bent-legged position for so long.

Thirty minutes later, she was still a little achy, but at least she and her sisters had made a tentative peace over sandwiches and green tea. Sami dragged her feet as they climbed the stairs back up to their workroom, but she'd promised to try again.

And this time, with the hour growing late, she'd agreed to focus on the pearls.

Tate stopped to pull the cord on her grandmother's dragonfly lamp. Night had fallen and the attic was dark. With the soft glow spreading over the floor, the three of them resumed their places.

"I'm going to keep my eyes open this time." Sami had her mouth turned down as she looked to the clock. "If we lose ourselves again, we may wake up on day two."

"So we'll watch each other," Fiona said. "That way, maybe we'll stay in the moment. Besides, we have to learn to control it at some point."

Tate wasn't sure what to expect since the three of them weren't joined together, but a snap of static was in the air. Residual energy rekindled when they all went to that relaxed place again.

But unlike earlier, the roll of power flowed freely, unrestrained.

Before, they had been a closed system. And now, without that physical contact, the magick they summoned whipped and cracked like a livewire out of control.

"Uh." Fiona hunched her shoulders forward in a defensive posture. "I don't like the way this feels. I can't find my core. I know where it is, but . . ."

"All the power is leaking out," Sami finished for her. "I can't get a grip on it."

Feeling unsettled, Tate spoke in a sharper voice than she intended. "Just focus, and try not to be so negative. That can't be helping."

Sami shifted her stare to Tate, the subtlety of the move a warning in itself. "You're not the editor here, Tate. You don't get the final say. You don't get to tell us what to do."

"I'm just trying to be reasonable." But the spinning forces scratched at her nerves, prodded her to add, "Someone has to be."

"Maybe that's the problem." Sami slammed her pearl onto the floor.

"Easy!" Fiona cried.

Sami didn't seem to hear. Or care. "You're trying to be reasonable. Fiona is overly emotional."

"Hey," Fiona objected.

"And I don't care what anybody says, I still have my doubts

about all of this."

"How can you not believe after everything that's happened?" Fiona grabbed Sami's pearl.

"I didn't say I don't believe. I just have my doubts."

If the magick had snapped before, now it began to roar, filling Tate's ears and rushing to her head. Her heart pounded, her hands burned. But she couldn't slow the growing chaos.

The energy in the room was bedlam. And the answering power inside of her blasted into a thousand slivers. "What's that supposed to mean, Sami? What doubts?"

"Forget it. It doesn't matter."

"No you don't, Sami. You don't get to take the easy way out and shrug it all off. Not this time."

Sami's expression contorted. The sound rolling from her throat was fury and pain, a dangerous mixture. "Oh, this coming from the sister who ran away when things got tough. Don't lecture me, Tate. You left your home, your family, and deserted the man you *supposedly* loved."

"Shut up, Sami." Tate threw down her pearl, paying no mind when Fiona gasped and chased the bouncing white gem, the precious gift, across the floor.

"You don't have to be a bitch just because you're hungry." A part of Tate flinched to hear the venom in her voice, but she couldn't stop. She added another punch. "You're just scared."

"And I know all too well that you *do* have to be a bitch." Sami's grin was like barbed wire. "Because that's just who you are."

Back from chasing the pearl, Fiona jumped in between them, making Tate realize she and Sami had both gotten to their feet. They were leaning toward each other.

Tate's hands were balled into fists.

Instead of cooling the situation like she usually did, Fiona only added her own fire. "The two of you are so childish, so selfish! You always have to go at each other without any consideration for how it affects the people around you. I'm sick of it!"

Tate heard Fiona's words. Her heart hurt to hear them.

But the stab of guilt only rolled into more anger. She'd lost complete control of her magick and couldn't get it back.

A power greater than them all had been unleashed, and now they were at its mercy.

"Just shut up, Fiona!" Sami yelled. "Why should we always censor ourselves because you're too weak to take it? The world isn't one big fucking cupcake."

"Don't yell at her!" Tate used one hand to push Sami's shoulder.

The return shove sent her stumbling back to land on her ass.

She was up in a flash, ramming into Sami like they were two football players on a field instead of in a sacred room surrounded by their family's priceless and fragile heirlooms.

But the rage still fueled her, guided her, and Tate drove her fist into Sami's stomach. Her sister returned by pummeling the side of her head.

"Stop it!" Fiona screamed. She drew ragged breaths, as if she were crying. "Stop!"

As Tate and Sami grappled, a sharper sound joined Fee's high-pitched screams. A terrible, ear-piercing wail. Sami used both hands to thrust Tate away, then clapped her palms over her ears.

Tate dropped to her knees, using her own hands to block the deafening sound.

All three of them tried to protect their eardrums from the shrill screech.

Tate panted as the pain overrode the throbbing in her face. The sound was far more punishing than Sami's fists had been.

Her eyes widened, clashed with Sami's.

When she saw the tears roll down her sister's cheeks, remorse crushed her. "I'm so sorry," she said, though she knew her apology wouldn't rise above the noise.

But abruptly, the clamor stopped.

Curling forward and putting her head to the floor, Tate fought back her own sobs. Her body shook, trembling with shame, the still-fading fury, and a slick, roiling nausea.

If this was what magick did to them, she wasn't sure she wanted it after all.

Whatever power ran through their veins, she and her sisters had steered it in the wrong direction.

At last, she slowed her breathing and lifted her head. "Sami. I'm so sorry. I don't know what happened." Her voice broke on a sob. "But that wasn't me."

"Oh, it was you." Sami stood hunched over, holding her abused stomach. "And it was me too. It was all of us." She indicated Fiona. "Those were our dark sides. And whatever force we just channeled took over our bodies, our inhibitions, everything. It made us say things we would never say."

"I know." Tate climbed to her feet. "I'm still sorry."

"So am I." Fiona wrapped her arms around herself. "That was so awful."

Sami released a shaky breath. "Yeah. And I'm sorry for my part too." She reached back, unclasped the locket, and handed it to Fiona. "But I can't take any more. Not tonight."

She shook the locket until Fee took it, and with her eyes still streaming, walked past Tate. "I'm done."

10

Bleary-eyed after a restless night, Tate tottered into the kitchen the next morning. She found her sisters had beaten her downstairs, with Sami brooding over a bowl of cold cereal and Fiona staring down at a frying pan.

"I was going to make French toast," Fiona explained without prompting, "but I can't seem to summon the desire."

Sami grumbled under her breath, then glanced up. And did a double-take. "Omigod, Tate. Your eye." She shoved away from the table and rushed to her sister's side. "Did I do that? Of course I did." Misery etched her face. "I'm so sorry."

Tate wrapped her arms around Sami and held her without words. Tension had persisted throughout the night but dissipated now with a simple hug.

When she pulled back, Sami rubbed her open palms up and down her corduroy-covered thighs. She was still nervous.

Tate would have to do something about that. "How about I make you one of my special omelets?"

"I love your omelets." Sami blinked like an owl. "You'd do that? After last night?"

"Don't be silly." Tate touched her eye and winced. "I think we gave each other worse when we were younger."

"True. And last night, we weren't completely in control of ourselves." Sami leaned her head to the side to study Tate's eye. "I'd feel better if you put a bag of frozen peas on that."

"It's not as bad as it looks." Tate moved to the sink to wash her hands. "Besides, I want to get started before Fiona changes her mind and decides her French toast takes precedence."

Dressed in fuzzy pajamas with ice cream cones scattered over pink, Fiona turned and wielded her spatula like a queen's scepter. "I command thee to cook yon eggs."

Tate squinted one eye. "I'm not sure that's right."

Fiona set down the utensil and wrinkled her nose. "I was never good with Old English. Or eggs, unless they were going into a batter."

"You were closer to Middle English," Tate said with a wink. "But no worries. I'll handle the protein." Smiling to herself, Tate opened the fridge to hunt for eggs, cream, and cheese. As she pushed aside a jar of pickles, she realized she was humming.

Magick lessons and quest aside, spending time with her sisters was therapeutic, healing in its way. Especially when it involved their special morning ritual. Rising earlier than Granddad or Brit, they'd often enjoyed an all-female breakfast hour.

Many a morning had started off with talk of boys, school drama, and other vagaries of teenage girls. So it was easy to fall back into that habit now, teasing, laughing, and bonding. While deep, dark secrets spilled alongside the milk.

Oh, the stories she could tell on them. And vice versa.

This was the real reason sisters remained loyal to one another.

Laughing at her own little joke, Tate's mind felt suddenly clearer, and she swore her body aches faded. As warmth spread to her cheek, she reached up to test the sore spot.

The pain around her eye had lessened.

Sami dropped her spoon into the cereal. "Tate. Wow." She pointed. "Your eye is getting better. I'm literally watching the bruise fade. What did you put on it?"

"I didn't do anything. Well, I didn't use medicine. But," Tate hedged, "I did look up a healing spell on the Internet last night, after I went to bed. I even recited the words three times as instructed."

Fiona froze in the act of dumping far too much sugar into her coffee. "But it didn't work."

"No."

"Not until now." She directed the sugar spoon at Tate, Sami, and herself. "Not until we were all together again."

Exhilaration bubbled through Tate. "We did magick yesterday, and Sami made fire." She did a happy two-step. "But this is still such a rush. I healed my own face. *We* healed it."

"I'm excited all over again." Fiona leaned against the counter. "And determined."

"Me too, Fee." Sami lifted a shoulder and smiled bashfully. "I really do want this to work for us. I want to fulfill Mom's last wish, whatever it turns out to be."

"Hmm. The key." Tate bent to retrieve two pans from a lower cabinet. "Maybe it unlocks a treasure chest. That would make me happy."

"Or a genie's lamp," Sami suggested. "To give us more magick."

"I'm going with the treasure, and cold hard cash." Fiona's response spurred surprised looks from her sisters. "What? It would make life better, right?"

"Can't argue with greed." Sami stood and headed for the coffee pot.

"While you're up, how about you make yourself useful," Tate inclined her head to the pantry. "Check to see if we have any—"

"Tarragon?" Sami spit out the word and blinked three times. "How did I know that? I don't cook." Her voice was hollow, an odd expression frozen on her face.

"You must remember," Tate said. "I've made this recipe before."

"No. That's not it." Sami slowly slid her gaze to Tate. "I heard your voice in my head." She put two fingers to her temple. "Like a distant loudspeaker, but definitely your voice."

"No. Couldn't be." Tate's laugh died when she met Fiona's emerald eyes, held her gaze, and clear as day heard her youngest sister's voice ask, *Why not?*

Tate shook her head and pulled on her ears. "Ooh. What is that?"

Fiona and Sami fixed each other with stares. After a moment, Fiona smiled broadly. She nodded as if in agreement.

Then they both broke into peals of laughter.

"What's so funny?" They transferred their attention to Tate, and suddenly their voices surround-sounded her brain. "Wait. Wait. One at a time, for pity's sake."

Sami laughed but stopped mid-chuckle. "Oh hell. Now we'll never have any privacy again."

"Yes, we will." Fiona waved a hand at her. "We'll learn."

Sami seemed to consider this, bobbing her head up and down. "Probably right. I just hope I learn to block this out before we bump into Jack again."

"Oh, yeah." Fiona made a face. "Neither of us want to hear *those* thoughts."

Images unbidden leapt to Tate's mind. She decided to beat them at their own game and visualized something really raunchy with a clearly-enunciated play-by-play.

Fiona's mouth fell open. "Tate."

"You asked for it."

"Seems to me, you're asking for it." Sami hiked a thumb toward the door. "Jack doesn't live far. I could drive you over now if you want to make that fantasy real."

Tate grabbed what was closest to her—an egg—and pulled back like an All-star pitcher.

"Okay, okay." Sami threw up both hands before ducking behind Fiona. "We'll stop."

"Or at least try to." Fiona brightened and stood on her toes. "Let's make it an exercise."

"You do that," Tate said, cracking the first egg into a bowl for emphasis. "I'll work on shutting you out."

"Sure. No more mind chatter." Sami put a finger to her lips and pointed from herself to Fiona.

Remaining quiet—both verbally and mentally—she and Fee rummaged in the pantry for herbs. A few blessed seconds of silence passed.

And then.

"For crying out loud." Tate whirled and put her hands over her ears, knowing it would do no good. "No singing!"

She returned to her egg mixture while the psychic duet played on. Sami and Fiona giggled in the closet. They whispered.

So Tate started humming again, but with more gusto, smiling at her little rebellion. She let the fork clink against the side of the bowl. Picked up the goat cheese.

And the fork began to stir itself.

"Guys," she said, and then louder. "Guys! Look at this."

The fork whirled as her pulse raced.

Fiona ran over, drew in a breath, and clapped with joy. The fork increased its speed.

"It's reacting to us. To our emotions." Tate took a moment to settle, to accept. She snapped her fingers. "Sami made fire when she was startled by the heat in her stone. A rush of fear, or at least shock."

"Yeah." Sami came up, watching the fork as it made her breakfast omelet. "This is very hocus-pocus. And I'm more weirded out by that fork than just about anything we've seen yet."

"The point is, the magick responds to how we feel." Tate looked to Fiona. "So *that's* how we learn to control it."

Fiona nodded, moved in to pat her shoulder. "Look what you did, Tate. All by yourself."

"Not just me." Tate's chest got all warm and fuzzy. "It was us. You two made me happy. You made me laugh." She put one arm around Sami's shoulders.

"Together," Fiona said, "we can do anything."

Tate sniffed and wrapped Fiona up with her other arm. Their connection, the bond of sisterhood, ran deep.

And that, she thought, was its own brand of magick.

"You aren't going to let it add the herbs too, are you?" Sami shifted wary eyes to the fork again.

"No." Tate nudged her out of the way and reclaimed—gently—her grip on the spinning utensil. "No one measures my herbs but me."

"We can move things." Fiona's eyes gleamed. "Telekinesis."

Crossing her arms, she reined in her excitement. "But I think we should keep practicing with the telepathy. Right now our mindspeak, objects and elements, they're all reacting to us. The magick, fire," she chin-notched to Tate, "the fork. We need to be proactive, and make things work when we *want* them to."

"Agreed," Sami said, trying for a second time to refill her coffee cup. "And hey, I heard on the news there's s special moon out tonight. Some planetary alignment not seen in a million years. Or something like that. Maybe it will increase our mojo."

Fiona gaped at her sister. She slapped her forehead. "That's it."

The urgency, the elation in her tone, had Tate facing her. "What's what, Fee?"

"Tonight. We have to try again with the pearls tonight." Fiona held up her hands as if surprised they weren't catching on. "Gather the moons?"

Fiona pulled the locket from beneath her pink pajama top. She took it off and returned it to Sami after safeguarding it overnight. "Why didn't the poem just say 'gather the pearls,' if that's all the goddess wanted us to do?"

Tate stopped herself from pouring the eggs into the pan and set aside the bowl, too caught up in the enthusiasm to risk burning the omelets. "Fee, you're brilliant. The lines, the words. They were so simple that we overlooked the obvious."

Sami re-latched the chain around her neck, and if Tate wasn't mistaken, stared down at the locket in apology for having given it away, even briefly, to someone else. "We should try the pearls while the moon is out."

Tate hated to throw a hitch into her plans. "But we tried last night. The moon was out then."

"But not directly overhead." Fiona made a noise in her throat. "What silly witches are we? Doing a moon spell inside the house."

Tate let the hope bloom again. "The moon, the actual moon. It's the missing piece."

Then she imagined how moonlight would amplify the power they'd summoned in the attic. They'd have to be certain before freeing a force that strong.

She remembered the fight last night, the hard feelings and angry words. The violence that had come so easily. A chill shivered through her bones. "We only try using the pearls if we truly feel ready and have command over our magick."

"So only after we've practiced with other, easier things," Fiona said.

Sami raised her mug. "And we only practice," she gestured to the still-empty frying pan, "after breakfast."

11

By lunch, Tate, Sami, and Fiona had mastered telepathic sending and blocking. Brit and Granddad gladly played guinea pigs, but no matter how they tried, the men couldn't hear or project thoughts.

Only the sisters.

After another meal—because working magick simply drained them—all three had successfully floated napkins, books, and even the now-empty cake dish in the air and over their heads.

Finally, with Sami's guidance, Tate and Fiona both summoned fire at will, flames leaping to their palms as if called home.

Now, the sisters three stood before the ivory-painted hearth, holding pure magick in their hands.

Each and every one of them burning white.

Once confident in this last ability, they decided to form a circle, to let the energy flow between them once again. With the fear of lost time lingering from before, Granddad and Brit served as anchors, ready to draw them in if they seemed to be wandering.

Tate easily pulled her power from her mind, just as Fiona tapped into her gentle heart. Sami rounded it all by channeling through her creative hands, blending her power with theirs to create the whole.

When their hands clasped, the magick rose, swirling through them, then outward and into the air. But this time the force was tethered, bound by their will, strengthened by their unity.

Tate shared a smile with her sisters, sent a silent message to them both, and then as one, they dropped their hands and broke the circle.

"I can still feel your magick." Fiona laughed, and she sighed. "It's separate from mine but still attached."

"I feel it," Sami said. Then to Brit, "How are we doing on time?"

"It's only been five minutes," her uncle told them.

"Good. That's what I thought." Sami drew a deep breath. "I'm going to reel mine in. See what happens."

Maintaining her own stream of magick, Tate sensed when Sami retracted hers. If the sensation of energy came in different flavors, the bold spice of Sami disappeared, leaving only Fiona's sweet and the piquant sharpness of Tate.

"I'll go next," Tate said. "You okay, Fee?"

"More than okay." Fiona spun in a circle, laughing as she moved her hands, dancing within the currents of magick.

Tate focused, opened herself up, and curled her gift back in to rest. "Whew. Not bad for only two days."

Fiona threw her arms up like a ballerina taking a bow and outlined a heart in the air before folding her hands over her chest. "I can't believe how much better that was. No screaming crystals or frenzy of errant magick."

"Much, much better," Tate agreed, "because we owned our emotions, and therefore, our power." As soon as she spoke, a yawn overtook her. She shook her head, caught another yawn in her hand, and marveled at Fiona as she flicked her fingers open to form twin balls of pristine fire.

"You have boundless energy, Fee, but I'm going to stop for a while. The moon rises in a few hours, and I'm tired. Too tired to be of any use."

"So am I." Sami stretched. "We've accomplished what we wanted to, but now we need to prepare for the real work."

"At the risk of sounding more and more like you, Sami," Tate slid her gaze to the sourdough sitting on the countertop, "I'd like to prepare—and *repair*—with grilled sandwiches and soup." She stifled yet another of the persistent yawns. "Then I really want to take a nap."

"That is a plan I can get behind." Sami shot two fingers to Tate. "I will even help slice the ham."

"I want to keep practicing." Fiona closed her hands to douse her fire.

"No." This from Brit, as he watched Tate yawn a fourth time. "Magick is hard work, and you three have already forced yourselves to advance in a short amount of time. Tate's right. You'll need to conserve your strength for tonight."

"The midday sun is waning now." Their grandfather stepped up to stand with Brit. "You can manage a few hours of sleep, so up to bed with you." He used his cane to point to himself first, and then Brit. "We'll make the food and bring you trays."

"But we only ate a little while ago," Fiona said. "I'll stay down here and—"

Granddad shushed her. "Go on. Go on." He shooed them with both hands. "No arguments.

Fiona rolled her eyes. "Three grown women who, I'd like to point out, can toss objects with just a thought, and we're actually getting sent to our rooms for afternoon naps."

"You'll thank me," Granddad said. He pointed at Fiona, "And no making flames in the bed. It's a fire hazard."

Fiona huffed, grumbled, and complained until she was upstairs and behind her closed bedroom door.

Three hours later, she was the first to say how refreshed she felt.

Already dressed in jeans and a thick sweater of Ireland green, she practically pulled Tate from her bed and chatted to her through the curtain for the duration of Tate's shower.

Together they went down to the kitchen to find Sami already waiting. She kicked back what remained in her coffee cup before setting it in the sink and rubbing her hands together. "Ready to do this?"

"Absolutely." Fiona gestured to Sami. "You have the locket?"

Sami gave a solemn nod, but behind her eyes, shadows lurked.

Tate recognized the anxiety, as it was the same shivering through her as well. They'd come to the end of the second day and needed desperately to make the pearls work, to take the next step.

Who knew how much of tomorrow they would spend searching for the key? That is, *if* they had any idea where to look for it. So they had no more room for failure.

The deadline was counting down, and their mother's simple words had yet to be put to use.

None of them wanted to let her down.

Silently they filed out into the cool night air, walking to the back expanse of open grass. Brit and Granddad waited for them there, their presence not only allowed but requested.

Tate shook her arms in an attempt to release the nerves tittering up and down her body and breathed to calm herself as she and her sisters circled up. Lifting her face to the moon, she gave thanks for the cloudless sky.

If the pearls did require moonlight, a veil of thick clouds could prove tragic.

As if reading her mind, Fiona said, "Let's get started before Hellana realizes what we're doing and sends a storm to block the light."

Sami pulled the locket from beneath her shirt and opened it to release the precious pearls—the "moons" left to them by their mother.

Both the disaster last night and the triumph this morning had taught them valuable lessons. How they approached magick could open channels or slam doors. The amount of power they wielded could be thrilling.

Or devastating.

Sami held the open locket out so Tate could choose her pearl.

There was ritual in having the eldest go first, and then Sami, before she let Fiona nimbly pick out the final white orb.

On this calm, cool night, the forest was unusually quiet, the wind light, and the distant ocean a low, insistent hum. Different from the last time they'd gathered in the back yard.

Still, instinct had them assembling with the pearls—and their wish for magick—around the scorched earth where the chest had rested for so long.

Tate clasped her tiny sphere within both palms. Sensing she should let love for family guide her, she thought of her sisters who needed her, her grandfather and uncle who'd always been there, and her mother, who'd been taken from them far too soon.

Emotion welled within her, flooding from the pictures in her mind and rushing to every molecule of her being, before zeroing in toward her palm, to the pearl.

Her sisters must have called their power as well, as a hypnotic radiance bloomed in the center of their circle. Pale yellow particles formed, burning like sparks. Floating, sweeping, they reminded Tate of bedtime stories and fairy lights shining in the deep, dark woods.

"It's working." Fiona's blissful expression was cast in a soft candle-like glow.

"Keep smiling, kid," Sami said, encouraging the positive energy they all knew they needed. But Tate could see she was trembling, her own smile straining as she stared at the lights.

Tate was quivering too, as the magick inside of her reached out and grasped an invisible force. What was in her pulled and stretched, fighting to overtake the energy that resisted.

Despite the autumn night and cold Atlantic breeze, beads of sweat popped up at her hairline, on her upper lip. Fatigue swamped her, but still she held on, bolstering her power. She gave her magick free rein to lock on to whatever lay just on the other side.

The other side of what? Or where?

"We can do this." Fiona bit her bottom lip and inhaled. She gasped when the canary yellow specks shimmered into orange.

The first trickle of the rebellious energy reached its fingers into Tate as the strong hands of her power began to triumph. "The source." That had to be what she felt. "The letter told us we had to free the source."

"I don't think it wants to be freed." Sami grunted, bared her clamped teeth, but then shot her gaze up to the sky with a faint cry.

Tate felt the same abrupt release as an indescribable sensation rushed into her, a flood of heat, of joy—of life.

The magick she had known before paled in comparison to the abundance that filled her.

Soon the glowing motes melded together into a streaming thin line. The leading tip circled over itself, making figure eights and other designs, like a laser at a light show. The dazzling streak twisted, spiraled, and finally flew straight up into the moonlit sky.

Tate watched, wondering if they'd lost it.

But the light returned to them, diving like a silent missile into the ground. The orange flare disappeared in the blackened soil.

"Oh, no." Fiona's expression went limp. "Did we do something wrong?"

"I don't think so," Tate said. "I can still feel the source." And she could. She'd somehow tapped into a hidden network, lines of energy that touched on every living thing as well as the inanimate. Rocks, water, creatures in the sky. Everything was connected, and so were she and her sisters.

They'd just never realized it before.

Tate continued to stare at the ground, unsure of what to expect.

Soon a squiggle of light appeared and began to undulate. At first, she wasn't sure what was happening, but then she saw it. "It's writing something."

The orange letters stretched and curled across the earth to form two words.

"*Hârtie spectru?*" Sami wrinkled her forehead.

"No idea." Tate shook her head and watched when more words formed below the first two.

This time it was Fiona who read aloud. "*Cerneală gândac.*"

As soon as the last words were scripted, the light vanished, blinking from existence.

"Quick. We should write that down." Tate worked with words every day, but these were foreign, unrecognizable.

"No need," Brit called out as he and Granddad walked across the grass. "That was Nadia's spell, all right." He stuck his hands in his pockets, grinned down at the soil that was again nothing more than dirt. "Our mother taught us Romanian. What you just read means specter paper. And beetle ink."

Tate handed her pearl back to Sami to place inside the locket and wiped at her flushed face. "Specter paper?"

"Yes, yes." Granddad shook his cane. "You'll need to make it yourself, but I believe the spell is in your grimoire."

"And the one for the ink too," Brit added. "You'll want to get started. The paper is no easy task."

"Nor is it quick," Granddad said.

Fiona lifted her hands and let them flop back to her sides. "Wait, wait, wait. Paper and ink? Another letter?"

"Just when we've solved the riddle of the pearls and gained even stronger magick," Sami said. "But I don't know if I can do any more tonight, even with the extra power. My body and my mental state are both tapped out."

Tate lifted her face to the cooling winds. "That was hard. Much harder than I expected."

Sami drew her long hair back with both hands. "Now it's the end of the second day, and all we have is another mystery."

"Mystery? What do you mean?" Granddad asked.

"We're running out of time," she said. "Making the paper and ink are one thing, but what do we do with them?"

"Oh, girls. I'm sorry. We should have explained." Granddad glanced to Brit. "Specter paper and beetle ink are only used together for one thing."

Tate's mouth dropped open.

Granddad chuckled. "You'll be making a map."

12

"Damned ghost paper." Sami blew at the hair hanging in her face and then proceeded to bat at the stray lock with both hands.

Tate stretched her aching back. "It's specter paper." Then in a tone meant to be soothing, she said, "Here. Let me," and tucked the stray auburn curl into the band Sami wore.

She understood her sister's frustration, though, because it swarmed in her as well. The grimoire lay open on the desk in the attic, and the spells used to create the required paper and ink were indeed inside.

These two particular spells, however, were in no way meant for beginners.

They'd readied all the tools and ingredients the night before—after Brit had made an emergency trip to Kat's store—but with eyelids drooping and bodies begging for sleep, they'd put off mixing the potions until this morning.

They'd awoken with an extra vibrant burst, thanks in part to the source they were now linked with. But eight hours and two failed attempts later, even that added dose of energy had been tapped out.

Tate and her sisters had just completed their second attempt at ink and paper but were hesitant to pour the stain on the page. On their first try, they'd forgotten a step while mixing the ink. The resulting concoction was incorrect, so dumping it on the paper ruined it as well, costing them hours of work.

Apparently, one piece of paper couldn't be enchanted twice.

"I think we've got it this time." Fiona tried for cheer, but her face was ruddy, and dark circles made her eyes look as bruised as Tate's had been yesterday.

"If we don't, we're screwed." Sami sat back to let Tate and Fiona do the honors. "Did you add the nickel powder this time?"

"Yes. I triple-checked." Fee blew out an exasperated breath.

Though the paper itself was store-bought, a heavyweight parchment measuring ten by ten, charming it into specter paper took time. Not mixing the materials, but forcing the spell into the paper with magick.

They couldn't afford to start over again.

With a gentle touch, Tate placed the enchanted sheet in a wide metal tray, one originally intended for photo development.

Hands shaking, Fiona lifted the special bowl. The container was fashioned of ball clay gathered only from certain swamps—thank you, Kat—and was specifically required for the proper creation of beetle ink.

Holding her breath, Fee poured the deep blue ink over the paper. She set aside the stained clay bowl but never took her eyes from the sheet in the pan.

Tate and Sami leaned forward to watch with her. So far, nothing was happening.

Just like the last time, when they'd messed up the ink. Tate chewed on her thumbnail, caught herself, and tucked her hands between her knees.

Another ten seconds passed and Sami whispered, "Come on. Please work."

Magick must have had heard her plea, because the paper slowly absorbed the ink, sucking it into its fibers as if thirsting for the indigo liquid. Soon the stain disappeared completely.

Tate and her sisters waited, staring at the blank page. They watched. Hoped.

Until the dark blue rose again to the surface, forming a border of flourishes in vintage design. Exactly what one would expect to see on an ancient map.

"We did it." Fiona grabbed Tate's hand, crushing her fingers as she squeezed. "We did it."

"It's still working, though, isn't it?" Sami pushed in between them. "That can't be all."

Another five minutes passed, but only the border had appeared.

"Let's take it to Granddad and Brit." Fiona wiped her hands on a towel and picked up the sheet by its corners.

Sami stuck a finger right in the middle and stroked the surface. "It's dry. Completely dry." She stood and slapped her thighs. "We might as well see what they say, because there's no time to make another."

Downstairs, the men were in the kitchen. Brit paced while Granddad sat at the table with his knee jittering and his chin propped on clasped hands. Restless concern oozed from every movement they made.

"We think it worked, but there's still no map." Fiona took the paper to Granddad for his inspection.

"No map?" Brit joined them at the table to study the paper. It still boasted nothing more than a fancy border. "But the specter paper works. I know it's called that, because images appear and disappear. I've never actually it in action, though."

"We saw the border take shape." Sami shrugged one shoulder. "But nothing else."

"Hmm. This is a worry," Granddad said. He gave a small shrug. "I've never done this myself."

Tate looked out the bay window. The telltale purple skyline warned of impending dusk. "We have until midnight to figure this out." She rubbed her forehead and turned to Fiona. "Maybe there's something more in the grimoire about how to reveal the rest?"

"I've scoured almost every page." Fiona crossed her arms, bit her bottom lip.

"Not only are we stuck, *again*," Sami said, "but we're all so tired. We can't face Hellana like this. She'll destroy us. Hell, I won't even be able to run if a bloodhound comes after me."

"What are you saying, Sami?" Fiona looked near tears. "We can't give up now."

"Oh, yes we can. The risk is too great." Sami threw out her hand toward the spot where Rhiann, the golden messenger, had appeared to turn their lives inside out. "We're given half of a message and are then expected to run off into the night to fight those bloody dogs that could rip our throats out with one bite? And Hellana, their evil mistress from another realm?"

"Brit and Granddad will be with us. Together, we can beat her."

"It's too dangerous. And why?" Sami continued to rant. "Some key to who knows what? All we have is a riddle from the goddess about happiness, magic, and our lives. We don't even know what that means, but we do know how dangerous Hellana is."

"You're tired," Fiona said, touching Sami's shoulder. "We all are, but that's no reason to quit. We'll take a break, get some food—"

"That won't be enough, and you know it. We're out of time, out of magick, and we don't know how to fix the map." Sami shook her head. "I'm sorry, Fee, but I won't risk my family for some sketchy, mystery reward."

"But we have to," Fiona objected. "Rhiann said this is our opportunity."

"For what, Fee?"

Fiona didn't answer, only dropped her eyes.

"We've worked tirelessly and have only run ourselves into the ground. If we try to go out there now, armed with nothing but a little white flame," Sami pointed to the door, "we're as good as dead."

Her sister's ominous prediction sent shivers down Tate's spine. Sami's argument, and her fears, were valid.

Hugging herself and rubbing her arms, Tate shifted to meet Granddad's gaze. He too remained silent, and she couldn't guess what he was thinking.

But what if Sami was right? What if they were killed? Or worse, what if only one of them came back? What if only she lived?

No. She'd already lost her parents. She couldn't stand to survive her sisters too.

Imagining that pain drove her to speak up. "Sami's right. The risks outweigh the goal. We don't have a clue what we're searching for, and our map," she indicated the paper, "doesn't work."

"So we're staying here?" Fiona asked, disappointment dripping from her tone.

"Yes." Sami's answer was like a slamming door.

And in response, the sound of a distant chime, the gong of some ancient bell, resonated through the kitchen. The bass-like vibration coursed through the house again and again.

"Am I the only one hearing that?" Fiona asked.

A sweet smell carried to Tate. She sniffed, searching for its origin. The air in the adjoining parlor seemed to be shimmering.

She rushed in but stopped several feet away from the apparition, blinking her eyes to clear her vision.

"I see it too." Sami was beside her, with Fiona and the men following.

A large oval shape formed, like a pool of clear water standing on its side.

"I've seen this before." Granddad made a sound of aggression in his chest. "Girls, step back."

Tate had only ever seen one thing anger her grandfather this way.

Emuirdane stepped from inside the liquid, but his onyx hair and clothing remained fully dry. This time he wore a cloak, his dark brows clashing and handsome mouth twisted. "I expected more from Nadia's children."

Eyes like shining bits of coal raked over Tate and her sisters. "Such cowardice."

Tate automatically positioned herself between him and her family. "You can't just enter our home whenever you please."

"I can, and I will. Until the day your family's debt is repaid to me."

"We aren't cowards," Sami said. She and Fiona flanked Tate, refusing to let her stand alone. "But we don't know where to look for the key. Our map isn't complete."

He clucked his tongue. "The map leads you only once you've begun to search."

"Oh, for the—" Sami looked to the ceiling. "Will one of you magick people just speak plain English for a change?"

Emuirdane pulled his shoulders back. He smiled. But his narrowed eyes betrayed his displeasure. "I shall speak clearly, dear Samantha. You and your sisters *will* follow the map."

He flicked his cloak back with a snap and lifted the hand that bore the ring with its great oily-stone. "You will seek out the key and the woman who has taken it, the same person who has foolishly stolen from me as well.

"I cannot locate Hellana. She has my fibula." He curled his hand into a fist until black oozed from between his fingers. "She hides herself from me. She uses my own power against me!"

"What is the key?" Tate demanded, trying to tamp down her fear. "You said you were our protector, but you threaten more than you help."

"Only you and your sisters can find Hellana." He evaded her question. "Everything rests on your ability to do so. Tonight. If you fail, I will lose much more than my family heirloom. And if *I* lose," he stepped forward, "you will suffer."

"We can't fight Hellana." Fiona lifted her hands to him, trying to reason with the angry Iele. "We've used up our magick. We can barely summon fire."

"If that is all that stands in your way, then by all means, let me assist you." Emuirdane used the fist that bled black and circled it around his other hand and the ring it bore. He spoke strange words in a low rumble and flicked the dark substance at Brit and Granddad.

Brit dropped to the floor, but Sami was able to catch their grandfather and lower him gently. "What have you done?"

Tendrils of light swirled from Brit and Granddad, white streaks that flew from their bodies and into Tate, Sami, and Fiona.

Tate's head and chest throbbed once with a great squeeze and release. Then her system jolted as power rushed from her center out to her fingers.

Her magick had been renewed, as if she'd been given . . . a new life force.

Terror swamped her as she fell to her knees beside her grandfather. He was so pale. She couldn't tell if he was breathing.

She looked up at Emuirdane "What did you do to them?"

He waved a hand. "They are merely sleeping. Very deeply. I have transferred their power and stamina to you and your sisters."

He leaned down and pushed the tip of his finger into her jaw. "I will not be disappointed, Tate Whiteburn. I will not be denied what is rightfully mine."

He stood again and wiped a hand down the front of his shirt. His voice was calm, almost pleasant, when he said, "You should make haste. You three will hold the essence of your uncle and grandfather within you until you have found Hellana. Then, and only then, will I allow your uncle and grandfather to awaken."

"What if we can't?" Fiona cried, overcome by doubt for the first time.

Emuirdane cocked a black brow. "You must. They cannot sustain this sleep for too long, or their spirits may be lost. Forever."

"Damn you." Tate cursed him through gritted teeth. She clamped her jaws until they ached.

"Yes, yes. Damn me." Emuirdane waved again, so unconcerned. "I've heard ten lifetimes of curses against my soul, and none have ever taken."

Sami stood. "Are you sure? Because you seem to covet many things."

"True. I might not possess it all now, but one day I will have everything I want." In a lightning-fast move, Emuirdane crossed to Sami. He ran a finger up her neck, and with this touch, evinced a very different vibe than when he'd threatened Tate. "*Everything I want.*"

"Don't touch her." Tate jumped up and shoved herself between him and Sami.

Emuirdane laughed and eased away, tapping his bare wrist. "Time dwindles. Would you save the lives of the men you love?"

"Please," Fiona begged.

"Follow your guide," he insisted.

"The map?" Fiona rushed forward. "But how?"

"I will have my stolen property by midnight." Emuirdane turned from them and re-entered the liquid portal.

His voice rolled back to them, deeper and wavering, as if traveling through water. "Or you will never speak to your loved ones again."

13

They decided Tate would hold the map. Each of the sisters had their daggers hanging from sheaths on their hips, but only Sami had hers at the ready. Fiona, with the most natural affinity for magick, kept her hands free in case she needed to draw and deliver fire.

Putting on coats felt silly to Tate, considering what they were up against, but the wind blew cold and hard as the sun set over Bar Harbor. And as soon as she stepped outside, she could tell the temperature had dropped considerably.

Sami huddled within her jacket. "Brrr. Do you think that's Hellana?"

"Maybe." Tate studied the full moon, the cloudless sky. "She hasn't sent us a storm. At least, not yet."

"Emuirdane said the map would lead once we begin to search." Fiona notched her chin toward the front of the house. "Out to the street? Maybe we'll have to drive."

They turned and walked three steps before the map reacted. Tate gasped. "Look." A blue dash formed in one corner of the paper and turned to brown. Then a blue beetle the color of the ink appeared, flashed once, and rotated in a half-circle before scuttling a few steps.

"Guess that's why it's called beetle ink." Sami scrunched up her face. "It walked to the line and stopped."

"What's does the line mean?" Tate asked. She took a few more steps toward the front yard, but the bug remained fixed in its position.

"This is confusing." Sami thrust her fingers in her hair. "Let's go back to the door where we started, and try going the other way until we can decide what the beetle's trying to tell us."

They did as she suggested and returned to stand outside the exterior kitchen door. The beetle didn't move.

They took a few steps toward the back lawn this time, and the tiny blue bug scurried across the map, leaving a dotted line in its wake. The sisters paused, and so did the beetle. They took several steps, and the bug moved again.

As the beetle progressed, vague depictions of landmarks materialized on the paper.

"It's leading us to the back. We just have to keep moving." Tate picked up her pace. With the ocean, cliffs, and forest represented on the map, she could anticipate the beetle's general direction.

She and her sisters headed straight for the charred pit in the ground, but the beetle made a forty-five degree left turn. Following its lead, the women angled to the forest lining the side of their property instead of the cliffs.

"We're going into the woods." Sami made the observation, but they all drew a collective breath. The forest meant shadows, darkness, and too many places for monsters to hide.

Autumn leaves crunched under their boots as they entered. Within the shelter of the trees, moonlight still reached the ground, but only in patches. Pale white cast wherever it managed to slip through the dense boughs of pine needles or naked branches of the hardwoods.

"Flashlight?" Fiona asked.

"Let's wait." Sami switched the dagger to her left hand, wiping her right palm on her pants leg. "We can still see pretty well."

"And the light could give us away." Fiona nodded, then added, "What about you, Tate? Can you see well enough to follow the map?"

"Yes, but it is getting darker." Another five minutes, and her words were made true. Heavy clouds slid across the sky to block the moon.

"Hellana," Fiona whispered.

A bloodhound bayed from deeper inside the forest.

Tate stilled as fresh terror paralyzed her legs. But she jumped, barely stifling a squeal when a flash of white fire streaked past her.

"Fiona," Sami hissed. "Careful you don't burn the map." She put her hand on top of Fee's and lowered it to a safe level, palm facing the ground. "Or us."

"Sorry." Fee's eyes were huge in her pale face. "I was startled. The hellhounds . . ."

"Don't stand a chance against my dagger," Sami assured her.

Fiona had every reason to fear the hounds and was probably flashing back to the night she'd been mauled. "But they should really be afraid," Tate took Fee's hand and raised it again, "of your fire."

Tate glanced to Sami who nodded. "That's right." She hiked a brow. "But watch that hair-trigger."

After standing still and listening for movement, Tate said, "I don't think the hounds are stalking us." No padded footsteps trampled leaves, no fog crawled the ground, and the moon was released from its thick veil of clouds. "Hellana is holding back."

"She's still storing it up for us," Sami agreed. "More power to unleash on us once we finally find the key."

As they walked, Tate looked to the map and made sure she was still trailing the beetle.

After a few minutes, Fiona spoke. "You know, I was excited when we first learned about the magick. Sure, because it sounded fun and exciting, but more than that."

She slipped her arm through Tate's, leaving Sami's free in case she needed to wield the dagger. "The ability, the gift, was something we could share. Let's face it, other than blood and basic physical traits, there's not much else we have in common."

"I know what you mean, Fee." Sami shoulder-bumped their baby sister. "We're more connected now."

"And not only to each other," Tate added, suddenly fighting tears—deep in the dark woods while trying to see what a little magick beetle would do next.

"We're closer to Mom too somehow." Fiona completed Tate's thought.

Tate sniffed and cleared her throat. "I know I don't say it enough, but I want you both to know—"

"We know, Tate." Sami stopped her, her own voice catching. "And . . . me too."

"Me three." Now Fiona did take Sami's arm, just for a second, and squeezed both her and Tate in close. "We'll make it out of this. We have to. Brit and Granddad are relying on us."

Tate leaned her head to touch Fee's, but when the beetle made a hard right, she slowed and pointed. "That way."

"To the cliffs," Sami said.

The sound of crashing waves grew as they neared the edge. The tide and crunch of dead leaves were the only sounds in the crisp, quiet night.

As they neared the deadly drop off, Sami said, "I hope that beetle knows what it's doing."

Fee laughed lightly, but the sound was tight with apprehension. "And that we can't fly."

Tate took cautious steps to gaze over the ledge and far, far down. Fortunately, when the beetle met up with the line marking the cliffs, it made another turn.

Tate did her best to follow its trail exactly, but she had to backtrack once before realizing the bug meant for them to walk down a path that cut across the bare face of the cliffs.

"I'll lead," she said, still eyeing the beetle. "You two get into single-file. And be careful."

Sami slipped then, sending loose gravel falling off the side. Fiona grabbed her, steadied her, and the two of them stood stock-still, breathing heavily as they looked wide-eyed to the ocean below.

"Careful. Okay. Got it." Sami exhaled and motioned for Tate to go ahead. They resumed the slow, cautious trek down the narrow trail. Pebbles tumbled and dirt slid, until a third of the way down, the path came to a dead end.

Tate paused in confusion, gazing out into nothing but salty air. The beetle had stopped moving, but was facing to the left.

She turned her head and studied what looked to be a porous wall of bedrock. Tilting her head, she thought she saw the surface morph. It flickered.

She stuck her hand out and retracted with an expelled breath when her fingers swept through the surface. Not solid at all, but an illusion.

Forcing down the nervousness, she held a finger up to her sisters. "I'll go first."

"No." Sami latched on to the back of her coat. "We don't separate. That only makes us vulnerable."

Sensing her determination, and noting Fee's stalwart expression, Tate nodded and slid her entire arm through the façade before stepping inside.

She entered a cave, rather, a corridor that seemed to be part of a tunnel system.

Her eyes adjusted, and so did her assessment. She hadn't simply entered a cave, but what felt like another world.

The shaft before them shone with a preternatural glow. Rocks were stacked into pyramidal piles and scattered at various points along the passageway. Bluish-green light emanated from the stones themselves, illuminating the path but leaving the ceiling in shadow.

"Creepy," Sami whispered, bending to get a closer look. She

jerked upright. "Something's in there, alive, in the rocks."

Tate studied the surface of the stones—from a safe distance—and saw movement on the surface. Phosphorescence?

"At least we can see," Fiona said. She tapped the map. "What's the beetle doing?"

Tate swore when she looked at the paper. "It's gone. The beetle's gone."

"Maybe it led us as far as it could." Sami scanned the dark tunnel ahead. "Or maybe stronger magick lives here. Hellana could have done something to protect her home just like Brit and Granddad did to ours."

"We've come this far," Tate said, rolling up the map and stowing it inside her jacket. "And based on the surroundings, we must be close to Hellana and the key."

"Let's push on then." Sami raised her dagger. "We don't know how long Brit and Granddad can hang on, and I won't lose them to Emuirdane's permanent sleep."

Tate edged forward. "Let's just hope the tunnel doesn't split."

For another several minutes, they were fortunate in that regard. The corridor curved and descended slightly, but the single passage remained. Finally the shaft ended, opening into a cavernous room with a pool of water fed by a glimmering waterfall.

On the far side, Tate noticed another lone hole in the wall. "There." She gestured. "That's where the tunnel picks up again."

"We have to take this path around the water." Fiona shot a fearful look to the oddly-glowing pond. The same lustrous rocks dotted the bottom, lighting the body of water with the strange aqua hue. "I don't want to fall in there. It's beautiful . . ."

"But deceptive," Tate finished. "I feel it too. We must be getting closer."

The atmosphere felt thicker, as if layers of magick had amassed in this room. She studied the beguiling waterfall, the mesmerizing pond.

Then something skittered in a dark corner. With legs that clicked.

"That wasn't a rat." Sami eased along the path, her back pressed to the wall. "I think I prefer the tunnel, so let's move."

Tate let Fiona go next and followed up close behind her, ready to grab either of her sisters if they lost their balance. The closer they drew to the center of the pond, the more she picked up on a floral scent. Sickly sweet, like nothing she'd ever smelled before.

Sami inched along carefully, but she sped up to get past the depths in the middle. There the bottom was absent any light, black and fathomless. At last, they found purchase on a wider shelf near the tunnel entrance.

"I've got a headache," Fiona said. "That water is putting off some kind of chemical, or poison." She tugged at the sleeves of her coat, pulling it off. "I'm hot. Are you hot?"

Tate took hold of her shoulders and steered her into the passageway. She could already tell it was darker on this side of the pond, but she had to get Fiona away from the noxious water.

"You're more sensitive to magick than we are, Fee." She waved her hand in front of her sister's face, then used the discarded jacket to cover Fiona's mouth and nose. "Breathe through this."

Sami ripped hers off too and did the same. "How do you feel, Tate?"

Stopping to worry over herself for a moment, Tate realized she had a sharp point of pain between her eyes, about the size of peanut. "A little headache. Not too bad."

Sami nodded, the coat covering the bottom half of her face, and continued down the tunnel.

Tate lost sight of her almost immediately. "Wait for us, Sami."

"Hurry," Sami called back from somewhere in the black.

Either Tate was imagining things, or the air was heavier here, denser . . . a force unto itself that literally swallowed light.

"Sami," Fiona called. When Sami didn't answer, she snapped

her fingers to produce a small white flame and tossed the fire into the air to brighten the shaft.

Sami was nowhere to be seen.

"Oh God, Tate. We have to find her." Fiona dashed ahead.

"Wait!" Tate reached out, her fingers literally locking onto the bottom of Fiona's green sweater, but that was the only part of her she could see. The rest of her sister had disappeared.

How could that be? She was only a foot away.

"Tate?" Fiona's voice was small and scared. "Is that you? How'd you get in front of me?"

Then Fiona screamed, and the ball of fabric in Tate's hand wrenched free. She stumbled from the hard pull, but quickly regained her balance and thrust her arms out, searching. "Fee!"

Rubbing her palms together, she created her own fire, enough to serve as a torch. Mimicking her sister's idea, she sent the huge ball of fire into the air. It lit the passageway for yards, but neither of her sisters was in sight.

She started to jog, distrusting everything she saw, afraid she would tumble into an abyss or be snatched away at any moment. Was this all a glamour? Was Hellana toying with them?

But Fiona's scream. What was happening to her sisters?

No! Nothing could tear them apart. They were closer now than ever, knew each other more honestly, and were bound by magick.

So Tate used one of their new tricks. She called out with her mind. *Fiona. Where are you? Sami?*

Nothing came back to her.

Tate was running now, taking the curves as fast as she dared, but still locked inside the single corridor. She rounded another bend and entered a straightaway. At the far end, the blackness quivered. She skidded to a stop.

Her torch had been leading her and was still yards ahead. Darkness advanced on her fire, and the thick, moving shadow engulfed the flames. Devoured all light.

Tate stood where she was, unmoving. She felt the blackness roll over her, through her. *Sami? Fee? Please talk to me.*

She heard a rustle somewhere ahead, and then the clicking. The same noise she'd heard at the pond. The sound increased, growing louder but also multiplying.

Whatever had been at the pond was here with her now, in the dark.

And it wasn't alone.

This time, she went full-on blowtorch, firing a stream of white fire into the shaft as Fiona had done in the forest. Fear amplified their magick.

Squeals and cries erupted as her flames struck.

Tate screamed too, and instinctively stepped back when hundreds of eyes reflected the brightness. Spiders? No, not spiders, but some otherworldly version of them. And huge!

She fired again as they screeched and lunged toward her. She shouted at them, setting her emotions free and filling her voice with all the terror, fury, and sorrow that had enveloped her over the last three days.

Her blast of fire scorched three of the creatures, and she stared, horrified, when they kicked onto their backs and waved innumerable legs in the air.

The clicking increased, grew to a clamor like a million knives sharpening. She wanted to cover her ears, but kept throwing heat from her palms, burning the disgusting insectoids.

One fell over before leaping back to its legs and scuttling straight for her.

Rage consumed Tate, and the resulting burst seared the giant bug. "Don't you touch my sisters!"

It was then she heard Sami's voice, but only in her mind. *Tate! Where are you?* Then she cried out. *Damn! I'm bit.*

Are you okay? Burn them, Sami. Kill them!

I am. I am!

Sami fell silent, and then, *I think the bite's healing, Tate. It's closing up, and the stinging's not as bad.*

Where are you? Do you see Fee? Tate destroyed the last of the creatures as it tried to attack. She charged onward, cursing the dark, determined to find her sisters.

No. She's not here. Sami's voice was strained, even as it carried to Tate's mind. *We can call her together. We're stronger when we work as one.*

Yes! Good, Sami. Tate drew an unnecessary breath and called telepathically, *Fiona!*

She heard Sami's cry echo with hers. Then again, they mentally shouted for their youngest sibling.

I'm here. Fiona sounded bedraggled, upset, as if she'd been crying. *Something grabbed me. It was horrible.*

The spiders? Tate asked.

No. It was a person, I think. But it had no skin or even muscles, just white and slimy, tendons bones . . .

Fee, calm down. Where is it now?

In a pile of ash.

Tate couldn't help smiling. *Good. Now we have to focus on one another. We have to find a way to come back together. Hellana's separated us for a reason.*

Sami's voice resonated with steel. *We can't let her win.*

We won't. Though she was in the dark, Tate closed her eyes and pictured her sister's faces. *I'm thinking of you both. I'm reaching out to you.* She sent her magick out in threads, searching for theirs to answer.

I feel you! It was Fiona.

She didn't hear from Sami, but Tate pushed, channeling all her strength to fuel the power they shared.

Fee, I've got you. Sami's relief came through loud and clear.

And the moment Sami connected to Fiona, Tate sensed them both.

And . . . something more.

What is that? Fiona asked.

Tate was right. Fee was the most sensitive.

It's not Hellana. Sami's voice. *The energy is good, positive. Is it something we created by joining together?*

Tate shivered when ripples of peace rolled across her heart. *I don't think so.*

Unlike when they'd tapped into the source, this new magick didn't pull against them, but gently coaxed. The vibe was warm, inviting, spreading through her with a softness that soothed and comforted.

Tate's chest tightened as her eyes misted. What was this? The goddess? Was she here to help them?

The Dea Matrona was a maternal deity who protected her chosen Matronae when they were most in need. Had she finally decided to intervene?

Follow it, Fiona said. *It won't hurt us.*

An aching sensation suddenly stabbed into Tate, the bittersweet sense of loss she so often experienced at home. This pain was the reason she'd left, and now it flooded her, reminding her of all she'd lost.

I can't. Her voice was weak as she sent it to her sisters.

Stay with us, Tate. It was Sami. *Please, don't leave. Don't let go.*

The grief squeezed Tate in a vice, tightening until she couldn't fill her lungs. Then as suddenly as it came, the ache shattered, allowing a burst of hope and light to rush in.

Sami. Fiona. Did you just—?

Yes! Sami answered. *Oh, Tate. It's so wonderful. I'm so happy I could cry.*

I feel . . . stronger. Fiona's thought bubbled with laughter.

Tate couldn't decide whether to laugh or cry. She was overwhelmed.

Her chest was too full, her head too sensitive. The pulses in her temples pounded like drums.

What was happening to them? She had no idea, but her gut told her this was no threat. The joy she felt was real and pure.

But how?

Tate opened her eyes.

And she knew. *It's the key.*

Throwing forth a ball of fire, she rushed forward again, navigating the tunnel at a near-run. The ground, the walls, none of it mattered. She couldn't trust her eyes.

But she had complete faith in where her heart was leading.

We're close, Sami said.

Tate could sense her sisters closing in. All three of them were drawn from three distant points, being pulled toward the same center, the same goal.

She now understood the cryptic words Rhiann had spoken. Everything made sense. The closer she got to the key, the more certain she became.

Up ahead, the corridor lightened. The dark void was giving way to something stronger. An open space was somewhere at the end, and it radiated golden light.

I understand! Tate sent the words to her sisters as she ran. *The key. The key will bring me happiness.*

The air around her brightened further as she closed the distance to her goal.

Sami's voice was in her head again. *And the key is the source of my magick.*

The tunnel ahead of Tate infused with glittering rays. This was it!

Fiona's voice was the last, and it was filled with happy tears. *The key gave me life.*

A starburst appeared before Tate, spreading from top to bottom and side to side of the tunnel. Without hesitation, she plunged into its light.

She stumbled through it and into a large cavern, just as her sisters entered from opposite sides.

Tate sensed they were safe, but all she could focus on was the key. A box of green glass lay on the dirty floor in front of a great hole in the wall. Beyond this place, whitecaps on the dark Atlantic glistened beneath the moon.

Inside the clear box, the key lay peacefully, its energy tugging at her. All this time, it had been so close.

The key to their happiness, their magick, and their very lives.

The key to everything.

Tate could barely breathe through the shock. She stepped forward, held out one hand, her voice weak and raspy as it trembled from her lips. "Mom?"

14

Tate dropped to her knees and laid her palms on top of the green glass. The woman inside was asleep, arms across her stomach like a fairy tale princess.

No air or sound passed from Tate's throat. Nothing could get past the mass of shock, the swell of love and hope. Her heart suddenly seemed too large for her body.

She studied the black hair, angled brows, and heart-shaped face. So like her own.

Her mother was inside the box. Her mother was the key.

"Mom." Tate skimmed her fingers along the edges and corners of the box, searching for a way to open the glass coffin.

The sound of crying rose in her ears. It wasn't until she felt a hand on her shoulder that Tate realized the mewling sounds were coming from her.

"Tate." Sami was on her knees beside her. Fiona stood close, tears streaming from her eyes, curled fingers pressed to her mouth.

Sami drew in a ragged breath. "Is it really her?"

Tate could only nod as sobs took over. She was thrilled, elated. Of course she was. But those words didn't fully describe the swell of emotions, the rush she was experiencing.

This was why she'd always felt her mother nearby, always sensed her spirit.

But how was she here? Why?

"Is she okay?" Fee asked.

When Tate looked to her, Fiona was a little girl again. Their baby sister who'd grown up without knowing a mother's love—the kisses that heal hurts, words of wisdom and discipline, or the special smile all mothers reserved for their daughters.

The fresh sense of loss washed over Tate, in crushing waves.

"Is she okay?" Fiona repeated, panic tingeing her voice.

"She is alive." A new female voice carried from across the cavern. "For now."

Tate looked over her shoulder. Though the woman seemed a bit more haggard than her depiction in the sisters' grimoire, Tate recognized the manner of dress, the jeweled chains draped around her neck and arms, and the ocean blue hair.

Hellana.

"You are stronger than I expected," Hellana said as Tate and her sisters stared.

The three of them readjusted subtly, forming a defensive line in front of the case where their mother rested. "What have you done to her?" Tate wiped at her cheeks, her eyes, clearing the tears to make room for hate.

She'd kill this blue-haired bitch before she touched their mother again.

Strolling around the dirty cave like a queen, Hellana tossed her hip-length hair back over one shoulder. She smiled.

"Answer me!" The base of Tate's skull burned, the core of her magick igniting. "What have you done to our mother?"

This time, Tate's demand registered with the Iele female. Hellana stopped walking and sneered. "What have I done?" She took two steps forward. "What have *I* done? I have been trapped here, beneath the ground, for twenty years."

She thrust out her arm, the sharp tip of one fingernail pointing to the box. "Because of her!"

Nostrils flaring, Hellana shot contemptuous daggers toward their mother, as if she could see straight through Tate and her sisters. "She put me here." Hellana spun, arms out to encompass the rocky warren.

Mid-twirl, she stopped with a jerk, narrowing eyes that were the same blue as her hair. "So I put her there."

"What do you mean?" Sami stood shoulder to shoulder with Tate and Fiona. "How did she put you here?"

"All this time, we thought she was dead," Fiona said before Hellana could answer. "She threw herself off of the cliffs. Our grandfather saw her."

"Yes, she jumped." Hellana seethed, pounding a fist to her chest. "She jumped to intercept me as I rose from the water. I had come to take one of her babes. One of you."

Spittle flew from her twisted lips as she spoke. "But she had worked a spell to protect her children. Her dear little *copii*. So she jumped, sacrificing her own life to strengthen the enchantment . . ."

Hellana paused. She stared into nothing.

One hand was poised in the air, fingers curling and uncurling. She hunched her shoulders forward and began to laugh. "But her spell, my magick, they clashed and mingled."

Hellana threw back her head and shook her fists at the stony ceiling. "And neither worked as we'd intended."

Tate glanced to Sami, and her sister returned her wary gaze. The woman was unhinged, cackling like a maniac.

"I gained my goal—entrance to your family's well-guarded lands—and your mother succeeded in keeping me away from her children." She flung out her hands again, her expression returning to one of fury. "And here we have remained. Trapped. Always trapped."

Tate's mind whirled as she tried to make sense of what the Iele woman was saying. This place, the tunnels, must be underneath their family property.

Though afraid to anger Hellana further, Tate still needed to learn more. She knew nothing of Hellana's magick or her mother's spell.

But she *would* free her mother. She would take her home.

After two decades of imprisonment.

She licked her lips and asked Hellana a pointed question. "If you've been here all this time, why haven't you come for us before now? Why not send the bloodhounds when we were younger and weaker?"

"Or why not try for us yourself?" Sami's words cut through the air. With the sharp edge of retribution.

"I told you. I am trapped here," Hellana snapped back at Sami, impatient, aggravated. "I borrowed magick to come to this world and mount my attack. My time here is linked to Emuirdane's fibula."

A shawl was draped over her dress, and she pulled it aside to reveal the fibula, clipped to the fabric at her waist. The silver was tarnished, the green jewels dark, as if oil swirled within each gem. The same as Emuirdane's ring.

The stones weren't glowing green as her grandfather had described. Perhaps they only shone for their true owner.

Hellana danced her fingers over the sickly green stones. "The fibula has been away from Emuirdane and his royal family for too long. It is leaching power, dying. When the magick is depleted, my spell and your mother's will break. I will finally be free."

"It's weakened already," Fiona said. "That's why you were able to send the hounds for us. And the storms, your laughter."

"Yes. And soon my physical self will be released."

"If you want to be free, then go." Sami marched forward. "You have no reason to hurt our mother, or us."

"Oh." Hellana wagged her finger at them. "But I do." Her mouth fell open, but she didn't speak. Instead, she looked about with a frown marring her deceptively beautiful face.

Tate watched her strange behavior. And then she felt the

riptide, an outward pull of magick as if all the energy was being sucked from the room. She glanced around, wondering what was happening.

The force rushed back in, swifter, harsher than the actual waves smashing into the rocks outside. A whistle of wind carried in from one of the tunnel openings, marked by a wisp of silver smoke.

Emuirdane stepped from the dark passageway. "Hello, Hellana."

If Hellana had seemed unstable before, she now became the picture of a madwoman. She clutched at the hair on her scalp and bared her teeth. "No! No! You can't be here! How did you find me?"

One side of Emuirdane's handsome mouth curved upward. His dark gaze slid to Tate and her sisters.

Slowly, Hellana's blue eyes followed. They widened with understanding. "You let him follow you here?"

With a growl, she reached into the many folds of her flowing gown and pulled out an s-shaped blade, gleaming silver and sharp on both ends. "I should have killed you in your cradles. You were always the greatest threat." Her entire body quaked. "I won't miss another opportunity."

Hellana raised the blade and bent at the knees to lunge. "Only one has to die!" She leapt, thrust high into the air with an extra push of magick.

But Emuirdane answered with his own power, catching her mid-leap. She hung immobile before he tossed her against the wall with a flick of his hand.

Hellana's head thudded against the rock, and she dropped to the grimy floor.

But she wasn't out of the fight yet. With surprising speed, she regained her feet and turned the blade on herself.

Emuirdane gasped and reached out a hand. "Hellana. Don't."

Tate looked to Hellana. She wasn't threatening to end her life at all, but held one point of the blade to the fibula.

"There's just enough essence left in this *seeleon*, dear husband. I will destroy your jewels, no matter the consequence."

"You would sicken yourself, just to destroy me?" Emuirdane feigned dejection, his lips turning down as if his feelings had been wounded. "Do you hate me so much?"

Though from a different world, a different realm, the spitting sound of disgust Hellana made was universal, and pure loathing. "If I can't take one of them from you," she gestured quickly to Tate, Sami, and Fiona, "then I'll take your precious stones."

Emuirdane's expression flashed. He morphed from simpering to furious in the space of a heartbeat. His hardened gaze held onto Hellana, but his words were directed to the sisters. "We can't allow her to destroy the fibula."

Tate drew her head back. What did he mean "we?"

"Why would we help you?" Sami asked. "You put Brit and Granddad in a sleep, a sleep that could kill them."

"Don't help him," Hellana hissed. "He lies. Always. He tricked me into becoming his bride." Hellana's expression shifted as she too tried to convince Tate and her sisters to side with her.

But the smile she offered the sisters was more of a grimace. "Just wait a little longer," she crooned. "The glass holding your mother will soon be gone."

"And she'll be free?" Fiona asked.

"Yes."

"No," Emuirdane said, his voice thundering through the enclosed space. "Nadia's glass prison will cease to exist. That part is true. Hellana's used the fibula's magick to create her prison and keep it intact, but as the power dissipates, so too will the coffin. And everything within."

Tate jolted. "Everything within? But—"

He locked stares with Tate. "If the magick of the fibula dies, so does your mother."

"No." Fiona's breath expelled with a burst. "That can't happen.

Please."

Tate swiveled her head back and forth between the two Iele. It wasn't a question of who to trust, but who to trust *less*.

Emuirdane's darkness was like a poisoned gas, always seeping out but never seen. He had harmful intentions. Of this, Tate was sure.

But not today. And he had helped them before.

Hellana, however, definitely wanted them dead.

"What can we do?" Tate asked Emuirdane, her tone steady, confident. Though inside she was anything but.

That spot at the back of her head still tingled with pent-up magick. Her instincts told her to call forth her power, to use it against the enemy.

"I must have the fibula." Emuirdane eased closer to Hellana.

In response, the blue-haired woman scraped the sharp edge of the seeleon across the stones again.

A groan erupted from Emuirdane. He put a hand to his chest, another to his cheek. "Now, Tate. Take it from her now!"

We have to get it, Fiona sent, moving a few steps out to approach Hellana from one side.

He could be lying. Sami put her hands back, touching the glass case as if afraid to leave their mother unguarded.

Stay there, Sami. Tate glanced down to the glass. *Stay with Mom.*

But, Tate—

If Emuirdane is injured, or if he dies, we don't know what will happen to Granddad and Brit. She turned her gaze to Hellana and sent her words to her sisters. *We have no choice.*

Hellana poked at the fibula and laughed at Emuirdane's responding scream of pain.

Fiona, Tate broadcast with her mind, *get ready to fire. Wait until I say.*

At Fiona's subtle nod, Tate moved toward Hellana from the front.

The woman's attention was on Emuirdane as she dealt her punishment with glee. "Now *you* are the one to suffer at *my* hands." Her ocean eyes danced as she tormented her husband.

Tate had the barest moment of sympathy, wondering how Emuirdane had hurt Hellana in the past, but she squashed the weakness. All that mattered now was getting their hands on the Iele jewelry.

All that mattered was their mother.

Ready? She thought to Fiona.

Yes.

Sami, Tate sent out, *when Fiona burns her, I want you to pull the fibula to you, to your hands.*

Okay. Sami widened her stance, still blocking their mother from Hellana. She breathed deeply, her shoulders rising as she prepared.

Another scrape on the green stones. Another cry from Emuirdane as he fell to the floor.

Tate stepped closer to Hellana, but the woman sensed her movement and realized Tate was advancing.

Tate lifted her hands. *Now, Fiona!*

Hellana's mouth fell open but before she could speak, the back of her dress exploded into bright white. Fiona's flames.

Tate shoved all her magick toward the fibula, concentrating on tearing it from the front of Hellana's dress and flying it over to Sami's outstretched hands.

She heard the sound of ripping fabric, saw a flash of blue as the fibula soared with a scrap of the gown still attached.

"No!" Hellana dropped the s-shaped weapon and stabbed her fingers toward Tate and her sisters.

But before she could attack with magick, Emuirdane hurled power from his outstretched hand. Still lying on the hard floor, he emitted a stream of silver from his palm.

The torrent of magick turned to thin silver ropes, the first cord wrapping around Hellana's wrists to bind her and halt her attack.

She grunted and shook her arms against the constricting ties.

More of the strands encircled her ankles, and then her arms, like metallic snakes strapping down her body. "Let me go. Let me go!"

Emuirdane climbed to his feet and dusted off his black clothing. He cast one last spell on his wife. He sealed her lips and stifled her curses.

With Hellana secured, he turned to Sami, held out his hand. "That belongs to me." His dark eyes shone as they fell on the fibula.

Sami tucked it behind her back. "First, you have to free our mother. Make sure she's safe."

Emuirdane lowered his head to stare from beneath his brows. "I can do neither unless I have my heirloom."

"Does this repay our grandfather's debt?" Tate asked.

"No. Both sides will gain tonight. You return my fibula, and in exchange, I give you your mother." Emuirdane rubbed his ring, the stone flashing as if it sensed the proximity of the other gemstones. "I need the power of your bloodline for an entirely different matter."

"Give it to him, Sami." Fiona motioned with her hands. Then the sweetest sister turned manipulative eyes on Emuirdane. "He knows we'll never help him if he lets her die."

Emuirdane gave Fiona a gallant wave of his hand. "This is true."

Tate felt sick at the idea of giving him more power, but he was the only one who could save their mother. "Go ahead, Sami. He wants us to be with Mom. She has to train us." She gave him a haughty look. "Our magick is all he wants."

"Again," he inclined his head, "you are correct." He snapped his fingers. "Now, quickly, before it is too late."

Sami didn't risk throwing the fibula but crossed to place it directly in his hands. She backed away, uncertainty still marring her brow.

The blackish-green stones revived as soon as Emuirdane

caressed them with a finger. The intensity within grew stronger, glowed with an unearthly emerald light.

Tate could see it now, beautiful but voracious. The same sinister power her grandmother had seen. And had known to fear.

Emuirdane whispered to the fibula. He shifted his eyes to the glass box.

The green case shimmered. Tate grasped Sami's hand, then Fiona's.

The glass thinned, lightening to a colorless sheen until finally, it disappeared. As they watched, their mother drifted to the ground.

Tate and her sisters rushed to her. With soft, tentative touches, they brushed at her cheek, her hair.

The lump was back in Tate's throat. "Mom? Wake up. It's us."

Their mother moaned lightly. Then her eyes flew open and she rolled to her knees. She was instantly alert, but her confused gaze flitted between the sisters.

"Mom, it's Sami." She gestured. "And Tate and Fiona."

"You've been trapped with Hellana for . . . a long time," Tate finished on a whisper.

With a shaky hand, their mother reached for Sami, caressed her hair. With the other, she cupped Tate's cheek. "My girls? You're grown?" Her deep brown eyes were huge against her pale skin.

Turning her head to the side, their mother released a short sob and leaned to place her hands on Fiona's black cap of hair. "Baby Fiona?" She drew a ragged breath. "You're a woman now."

Air fluttered from Fiona's lips as tears began to pool. "Mom. I've always wondered what your voice sounded like."

Sami gave a cry and threw her arms around their mother, then Fiona, and lastly Tate. Oblivious to Emuirdane's presence, she embraced her family, she accepted the impossible.

Her family. Healed. Restored.

Tate didn't know how long they clung to each other, crying and expressing disbelief again and again. She was still in awe, and her heart had yet to settle back to its normal rhythm.

Across the cavern, Emuirdane cleared his throat. "My wife and I shall take our leave, so you may enjoy this happy reunion."

Tate waited, held her breath, sure some terrible new development was coming. But the Iele only bowed his head. "You have completed your quest and have earned its reward. You will also find the men of your family whole and hearty upon your return home."

With a firm grip on Hellana's arm, Emuirdane moved to face a stone wall, dragging his runaway wife with him.

Lifting his hand, he rotated it in a circle. A silvery fog began to ooze from the rock until a sparkling mist covered the expanse. Emuirdane called out in a strange language.

A male voice answered from the other side.

Emuirdane spoke low in Hellana's ear before shoving her into the silver. She disappeared, lost in the glittery vapor. Her scream faded as if she'd fallen down a shaft.

Turning back to Tate and her sisters, Emuirdane looked to each of them as he said, "Rest. Study. Prepare. Take time and learn from your mother." With both hands he tossed the sides of his cape back. "For I will call upon you again."

For the debt, Tate thought. But what would he expect from them?

His serpentine smile formed, and he bowed with grace. "Until I see you again, consider this my parting gift." He put his hand over the silver and green-jeweled fibula, now throbbing with a resurgence of magick.

Tate watched his every move with caution, waiting for the trick. But as she stared, light rushed past her, streaking so quickly she could see nothing else. The brightness blurred into streaming lines of brown and gray.

Her head spun, so she closed her eyes. The sensation of movement overwhelmed her, but she could smell the metallic scent of rock, the rich loam of earth.

Suddenly, there was the salt of the sea, and she opened her eyes to midnight black.

Dizziness ravaged her, and she covered her face, breathing deeply to get her bearings.

Somewhere close, Sami groaned. "What did he do to us?"

"He brought us home," Fiona said.

Tate looked to see that it was true. The four of them were standing in their back yard. The cavern ceiling was gone, replaced by the dark autumn sky.

"Home," she whispered, reaching for her mother's hand as the world blurred from her tears.

Another group hug ensued. Tate laughed. She cried some more. This was a reality that would take some time to get used to.

But she would love every minute.

"Nadia!" Brit's voice carried across the yard. He stood with eyes wide as Granddad appeared beside him.

Their grandfather didn't speak. He simply held out his arms as his face crumpled.

Their mother rushed to her father, with Tate, Sami, and Fiona close behind. Brit put an arm around his father's shoulders.

Tate had never seen her uncle cry, but he did now. He reached out to trace the cheek of his sister, the one he thought he'd lost forever.

Hugs were exchanged amid soft cries, but soon excited chatter erupted. Brit and Granddad fired questions as Tate and her sisters promised answers.

They all stood beneath the watchful moon, happy, unbelievably blessed, and filled with the miracle of their loved one's return.

Emotion rose in Tate, a tidal wave of happiness, life—and magick. The three things that had healed the pain, that had saved them all.

"I want to come home." Tate's eyes drifted to Sami. "I know that I left you once." Her voice broke. "But I came back, and I want to stay."

Fiona put her head on Tate's shoulder. Then Sami reached out and pulled them both into her embrace. As they united, brilliant white light flowed up and spiraled into the sky.

Tate heard her mother's surprised laughter, and smiled.

With her cheek pressed to her sister's curls, she heard the emotion in Sami's voice as she drew a breath, squeezed hard, and whispered, "You'd better."

SUZA KATES

CALL TO THE EAST

WATCHTOWER MAIDENS

PROLOGUE

8 p.m. and all was quiet. In a research facility just west of New Orleans, Dr. Macario Thorne stepped inside his personal security room. The automatic door closed behind him with a hiss.

Easing forward, he took time to examine the monitoring station, pleased to see each room shadowed and inactive, the only light emitting from exit signs or sleeping electronics. Outside, the grounds were desolate as well. The vacant brick buildings appeared rigid and bleak, and even the ancient live oaks stood hauntingly still, absent any breeze from the rolling Mississippi.

Given the hour, all staff had long vacated the premises. Good little workers serving the watchful giant. A powerful giant known as Armistice, with a governing body and corporate face.

In his time working for Armistice, Thorne had made a quick and efficient rise in the hierarchy. He'd been named Director before his thirty-fifth birthday, but the honor of the position had always been marginal to his mind.

Of all the properties and pursuits regulated by Armistice, the sterile domain over which Thorne ruled was akin to little more than a bastard child.

The corporation's dirty little secret.

Movement drew his attention to two figures slipping through a darkened laboratory.

He watched them skulk, and his thin smile formed in the blue luminescence of the security room.

He had secrets of his own.

The couple, a man and woman, entered a hallway leading to the Venom Immunochemistry lab and its adjoining herpetarium. This area was isolated for safety reasons, entry permitted only to those trained in the handling of poisonous reptiles.

Dr. Purvil, with her silver hair cut short as a man's, used the keycard on her lanyard to gain access. Thorne had granted her a higher clearance level, one he allowed her in exchange for her contributions to his special projects.

As she and the man with her navigated the herpetarium, Purvil tucked her arms close to her body and away from the shelving units. She avoided getting too near, lest she brush against any of the glass cages and disturb the coiled serpents inside.

Purvil excelled in her subcellular field of science, where all things were tiny and neat, easy to control. Thorne had needed her particular expertise and so had invited her to join his cause.

Dr. Purvil desired prestige and, above all, greater recognition. For these reasons, she had agreed.

Still, she remained uncomfortable with the full-scale results of what they'd achieved over the last two years. As their studies yielded more advanced outcomes, Dr. Purvil seemed to grow more nervous. She'd also become increasingly evasive, allocating fewer and fewer hours to their clinical trials.

Still observing their movements onscreen, Thorne waited for Purvil and her research assistant, Ruark, to enter the storage room in the back of the herpetarium. Once there, they made their way to a sleek black cabinet with a permanent lock.

Thorne retrieved a remote from his pocket, and with a flick of a switch, the motorized cabinet slid to one side. Purvil and Ruark were familiar with the routine, stepping through before the faux piece of furniture moved back into place to conceal the doorway again.

Behind the walls, there existed an entirely different type of laboratory. Here, in the silent and undisturbed evenings, Dr. Thorne and Dr. Purvil used their knowledge to push and manipulate the boundaries of natural science.

Hidden entrances. Codes. Walled off areas obscured to everyone else. Discretion was vital, not only because the work they performed here was unorthodox. But also, and more importantly, their experiments were unsanctioned.

Thorne left the security room and traversed a corridor lit only by the crimson glow of emergency runner lights along the floor. He would meet up with his guests in the testing lab where they usually worked, a perfectly-calibrated and regimented space he found rather soothing.

Once inside, he paused to appreciate the cleanliness and organization. Beakers and tubes lined up like soldiers, steel worktables gleamed beneath luminaires, and ethanol freshened the air.

The heavy tread of another ruined his tranquil moment.

Purvil crossed the room in a clipped stride, as if in a hurry to be done with the night's business and on to better—perhaps safer—pursuits. Ruark strolled several steps behind her, apparently unmotivated by his supervisor's haste.

Like Thorne, Ruark had brown eyes and black hair, but where the younger man's features were rough yet handsome in a way women desired, Thorne's face leaned toward hawkish. In addition to gaunt features and eyes once described to him as "predatory," Thorne's physique appeared lanky because of his height.

But underneath his white coat, his body was in prime physical condition. Despite impressions, he was strong. Lean and tight, like surgical wire. Or, he thought with wicked pleasure . . . like a garrote.

After Purvil's recommendation and Thorne's approval of his involvement, the assistant had proven himself trustworthy, intelligent, and above all—ruthless.

This last characteristic, Thorne approved of most of all. A kind of viciousness danced behind Ruark's eyes, a rage in desperate need of purging.

This was where the two men connected. Where they understood each other.

Thorne touched the scar beneath his chin, the only disfigurement remaining after innumerable plastic surgeries. This particular cut had been too deep, the destruction of flesh too severe, leaving behind a slight dimpling of the skin. The imperfection would forever serve as a souvenir.

A reminder of innocent blood shed.

"Why the sudden meeting, Dr. Thorne?" Dr. Purvil's question was brisk, her jaw clenched as a sign of her annoyance. Her obvious wish to be elsewhere. "I do have other demands on my time," she continued. "My work on anti-inflammatory nanomolecules is to be published—"

"It can wait." Thorne's tone was sharper than normal, but her equivocation had become a frustration of late. An issue he must address.

He was darkly pleased when her eyes flared, and though she was quick to shutter her reaction, Thorne caught a glimpse of her unease, a flash of apprehension.

"The serum is ready," he said without preamble.

Purvil's expression fell slack with surprise. Her chin wobbled but she didn't speak.

Beside her, Ruark grinned.

After a heavy swallow, Purvil straightened her spine and rolled her shoulders. "How can you be sure? We decided to postpone further testing for the time being."

The corners of Thorne's eyes tightened. "No, Dr. Purvil. You suggested." He breathed out through his nose. "*I* decided."

Pursing her mouth, Purvil shifted her weight from one side to the other. "Your proposed plan is too dangerous. We should wait a little longer. When we reveal our work, we should choose something safer. Something more . . . subtle."

"Subtlety is too easily ignored," he countered.

"Exactly what I mean." Purvil wrung her hands. "You'll give us away if your serum works." When Thorne only stared, unmoved, she flung her hands out as her face mottled with pink splotches. "You'll bring them all down on our heads!"

Thorne remained impassive while Purvil walked in a small circle, still wringing her hands and occasionally mumbling under her breath. He counted seventeen unproductive seconds until his colleague managed to calm herself.

At last she returned to stand with Thorne and Ruark. Eyes skimming around the lab, she released a querulous sigh. "How exactly do you plan to proceed?"

"Come with me," Thorne said, turning to make his way to a solid metal door designated in red block letters as the Treatment Area. He punched in the required code on the number pad—silent, no needless beeping—and without revealing anything more, led the others to a section they'd never before been invited.

A long, narrow chamber expanded before them, a wide, empty passageway with a cement floor and individual rooms lining both sides. Each of the cells—Thorne thought of them as procedure rooms—was equipped with security doors and viewing windows made of ballistic glass.

As with the rest of his undisclosed workspace, he'd designed the procedure rooms himself. Per his direction, the windows were unbreakable. The cells impenetrable.

He stopped in front of one of the darkened cubicles. Once his associates drew near, he flipped a switch on an exterior control panel, illuminating the small cell.

Inside, an unconscious man lay on a stretcher. At the head of the bed, an IV pole held a liter of saline and two smaller bags, all attached to a delivery system.

Purvil gasped, recognizing the bag of bright green fluid connected to the pump. "You already have a specimen chosen? You have him hooked up?" She whirled on him. "What is this, Thorne? You didn't confer with me first."

"No, I didn't. No further discussion was needed." He ignored her growing anxiety and studied the slumbering man instead. Then he pushed another button to stop the flow of sedative from the second bag.

The amount of medicine didn't matter, though. Once the serum was administered . . .

Nothing would put the man back to sleep.

Thorne eased his hand to yet another button.

"Wait!" The pink arrow tip of Purvil's tongue flicked out to wet her lips. Her eyes darted back and forth. The pulse point at her temple throbbed.

Her level of distress only confirmed Thorne's suspicions. She was going to back out. Her weak mind was changing right in front of him.

"I support your agenda," she whispered, "but this isn't the way. It's too drastic." Her eyes locked onto the control panel. She lifted her arm, trembled as she reached forward, but finally dropped the limb to her side again.

Purvil was afraid. Yes, she was terrified of Thorne, and especially of what he was about to create, but there was something she feared even more. The ruling Goliath that was Armistice.

Disdain for the woman rushed through Thorne. What a terrible waste of intellect.

He tightened the muscles of his stomach, refusing to show any outward emotion. Still facing the window, he hovered over the button that would initiate infusion. Then he pressed. The IV pump began its digital measurement of the flowing serum.

"No!" Purvil squawked. "You fool! You condemn us all!"

"Deborah," Thorne said, his tone soft, almost intimate, "you're going to be a problem, aren't you?"

"What?" Her breathing was raspy now, shallow and labored. Her eyes were wilder still, and the artery at her temple hammered. With a quick shake of her head, she took a small step back.

Thorne turned to meet Ruark's gaze.

The other man gave a barely-perceptible nod before swooping in behind Purvil. He looped his arms through hers and held her in place.

"What are you—? Stop! What are you doing?" She struggled to wrench free, but her assistant was much stronger. Even as she thrashed and bucked, as she mewled for release, Ruark ushered her toward the cell with a dispassionate expression on his handsome face.

Thorne pushed another of his handy switches, and the air-locked panel slid to one side.

Purvil's low moan was thick with denial but rose to a sharp cry when Ruark shoved her through the open door. She stumbled toward the stretcher, righting herself by grabbing onto the rail.

But as soon as she regained balance, she froze. She took one cautious step away from the sleeping subject, and cast a horrified glance to Ruark and Thorne.

She held out a beseeching hand, as the door whooshed shut and sealed her inside.

Thorne and Ruark each chose an observation window. Purvil folded her hands gently across her abdomen. Her chest heaved. Her entire body quaked. But she didn't make any overt motions.

Until the man on the table opened his eyes.

Purvil began to scream in earnest, the shrill sounds intensifying to high-pitched shrieks.

From their positions of safety, Thorne and Ruark observed the subject interaction in the calm, clinical manner of the scientists they were. Even when Purvil started pounding for release. When inhuman growls filled the cell.

And even still . . . when droplets of red splashed against the unbreakable glass.

Ruark was the first to speak, in a voice buzzing with awe. "Would you look at him go."

"Yes." Thorne's chest felt swollen. Pride? Or anticipation? "He is perfect. I knew he would be."

Ruark pressed the tip of his finger to his window, tracing a bloody rivulet. Neither man spoke again until Purvil's screams decreased to gurgles and, at length, fell silent.

Ruark tapped the glass, his brows knit in concern. "Dr. Thorne, are you certain he can be controlled?"

"Of course. This initial frenzy is to be expected. The hunger is at its strongest upon waking." Again, Thorne touched his scar. "The craving is said to be . . . overpowering."

Ruark crossed his arms, still peering into the cell. "It's good that we gave her to him. Don't you think?"

Thorne smiled his thin smile again. He and Ruark truly thought alike. "I do. A fitting prize. After all, he is the first."

"What she said was right, though." Ruark thumped the window. "They won't understand at first, but eventually they will. They'll look our way."

Gritting his teeth, Thorne pictured the board of cowards who sat at the helm of Armistice. The inept figureheads who somehow continued to be re-elected.

The organization's very name incited him, referring to the all-important cease-fire. To a mutual truce. To *peace*.

But he knew better. He knew peace was just a lie fools told themselves.

While their enemies prepared to strike.

"Let them look. Let them come. The ranks of Armistice aren't as stalwart as they believe. Their complacency has ensured an inability to defend the organization, or anyone else."

"And that's the whole point." Ruark gave him a wolfish grin.

"Yes. The point." Thorne slid his gaze back to the carnage now spattered around the once-pristine cell. "This city has known peace for too long."

Suza Kates writes both paranormal romance and romantic suspense. She lives in Savannah, Georgia with her family and four ridiculously spoiled cats.

For more on Suza and her books visit

www.suzakates.com